"Step aside,

Rocco turned and ____ ____ one of fear. "I said ____ ____ will not be marryi____

The words were li__ a gut punch. She stepped forward to tell him off.

"Yes," Rocco said, his voice shaking just slightly. "I am."

Well, he'd tried.

"You're not," Apollo said. "You have two choices. I either expose your true identity and call the police, or you take the payoff I'm offering."

Hannah could only stare. She had been duped. And because of that Apollo was winning.

"I don't..." Rocco looked between Hannah and Apollo.

"What is this?" she asked, feeling sad, defeated.

"I'm sorry," Rocco said.

"I..."

Apollo shoved him aside and stood right in his place. It was as if Rocco had never been there at all. "You know, Hannah, I considered picking you up and carrying you off down the aisle. But that seems like a bit of too much melodrama, don't you think? I think perhaps I could save everyone time by moving into my rightful place. Here. As your groom."

"What?"

"Oh, yes. Your plans have changed. You're marrying me."

Millie Adams has always loved books. She considers herself a mix of Anne Shirley (loquacious but charming and willing to break a slate over a boy's head if need be) and Charlotte Doyle (a lady at heart but with the spirit to become a mutineer should the occasion arise). Millie lives in a small house on the edge of the woods, which she finds allows her to escape in the way she loves best—in the pages of a book. She loves intense alpha heroes and the women who dare to go toe-to-toe with them (or break a slate over their heads).

Millie Adams

THE FORBIDDEN BRIDE
HE STOLE

HARLEQUIN

PRESENTS

Recycling programs
for this product may
not exist in your area.

ISBN-13: 978-1-335-59234-7

The Forbidden Bride He Stole

Harlequin Enterprises ULC
22 Adelaide St. West, 41st Floor
Toronto, Ontario M5H 4E3, Canada
www.Harlequin.com

Printed in U.S.A.

THE FORBIDDEN BRIDE
HE STOLE

CHAPTER ONE

HE WAS GOING to kill her.

This was just another stunt in a long line of stunts Hannah had pulled over the past six months threatening to drive Apollo over the edge. And Apollo didn't do the edge. He'd been over it before. Hell, he'd been born over it. He had no intention of going back again.

Least of all, because of a bratty twenty-two-year-old whose well-being was his responsibility.

Taking Hannah in was the only good thing he'd ever done in his life. Everything else had been for his own benefit. Either financially or to feed his own depravity.

He was a strict guardian. When Hannah's parents had died, she'd been a straight A student on the path to certain success. He'd wanted to keep her there. At sixteen, she'd had two years left of high school. She'd gone to a boarding school, and he'd checked in with her often, his best expression of appreciation for the friendship her father had given him—another relationship that he supposed had become about more than what he could get from it—was to make sure Hannah carried on how she might have if they'd lived.

Her finances were in a trust that not even he could access until she was twenty-five or married. He paid for her life while she was in his care, and while he gave her a decent allowance, he wanted to make sure he kept her focused on her studies.

She'd done well. She'd graduated top of her class in high school, then gone on to university, where she'd studied technology and hospitality, which put her in a unique position to work for her father's hotel brand and liaise with his tech company, implementing unprecedented smart tech into the luxury resorts.

That was a reflection of a job well done.

He hadn't allowed her excess funds because he felt that would lead to others taking advantage of her. It would be a distraction. Even when she was in university, he made his expectations clear. No parties. No dating. No drinking.

He'd never had the chance to have an education, and it felt good to see her have a top-tier one he ensured she took seriously.

All had been well until she suddenly had a

personality transplant after graduation. She had been living with him since vacating her college dorm, lacking the money to afford her own lodging but apparently making plenty enough to be the life of the party. She had gotten a job—but not at her father's company. At a competitive hotel chain, not as an executive, but as a concierge. She'd suddenly developed a taste for nightclubs, parties, and staying out late.

Last night he'd told her in no uncertain terms was she to go out tonight. And it was past 2:00 a.m., and he'd gone in to check on her, and she was gone. It was rare for him to be bested by anyone, let alone a near child.

The issue was that he hadn't treated her as a prisoner.

He would now.

Until she was twenty-five, she was his ward. Perhaps he should have expected this. Perhaps it was unavoidable that her trauma over her grief would eventually turn into a meltdown of some kind. Was it not his job to protect her from this also?

That was when he heard scrabbling outside. Coming nearer to the second-floor library where he sat, drinking a scotch. He knew she would pass through here because he'd figured out it was how she was sneaking out.

So, he'd decided to lie in wait.

The window opened, and in she tumbled. Ingloriously. Shoes in hand, a dress so short it was more like a glittery T-shirt. She stood straight, her hair cascading in a tumbled, curling mane around her shoulders. The dress left nothing to the imagination. Her curves were out, on full display. And Apollo saw red.

"What the hell are you playing at?"

Hannah was frozen to the spot, pinned by his dark magnetic gaze. Even in the dim firelight, she knew his features, all too well. The sharp cheekbones, the square, granite jaw.

His heritage was Greek and Italian, but he had always put the marble statues to shame. He was broad and tall, well-muscled. She had a map of his body drawn out neatly in her mind, and she could refer to it whenever she wished. She did more often than she'd like to admit.

She'd had a crush on him from the time she was fourteen. When she was sixteen, he'd become her guardian. If those weren't the most confusing, mixed-up authority figure issues, she didn't know what was.

Worse still, from there her crush bloomed inside her and grew like ivy, wrapping itself around every part of her, turning into devastating, paralyzing love.

Now in her twenties, Hannah understood

how it had happened. Apollo had been an object of fascination to her already. Then when her parents had died, he'd become her everything. The one who was taking care of her. The one she found most beautiful. The one who had known her most of her life. The one who had known her parents.

Not loving him would have been an impossibility. Loving him was too, though. The more she understood her feelings, the way things were between women and men, the more she resented the dark pull he had on her.

Because at fourteen she'd wanted to marry him. At sixteen she'd wanted to give him her virginity. She'd had foolish fantasies of trying to seduce him—which in hindsight made her cringe because he'd have sent her packing and rightly so.

But now, at twenty-two, she wanted to be consumed by him. Her fantasies were no longer hazy and romanticized. She recognized that what she wanted from him was everything.

It was an obsession.

Also unhealthy. Also why she was desperate—so desperate—to recast her role in his life? To gain her independence. Because how else was she ever going to exorcise these unwanted emotions and needs?

Her whole body went tight with him sitting there.

She hadn't been expecting this.

Not quite, anyway. She was sure Apollo knew she'd been sneaking out because she knew her guardian well enough to know he wasn't an idiot. And he ought to know her well enough to realize she wasn't either.

She hadn't wanted to try to swan past him out the front door, but she had wanted him to notice that she wasn't behaving like herself.

Or maybe she was.

She'd made friends at her new job, and those friends had very plainly and loudly let her know what they thought about her life: That it was effed up.

When she'd explained her situation to the other students at her private university, they'd found it odd, but they'd understood on some level. Because her parents had been wealthy, and Apollo was rich. And it was accepted that rich people handled things differently.

Her friend Mariana thought it was outrageous and hideous and that Apollo was a gargoyle.

And worse, Mariana saw through Hannah and had seen through Hannah, to her most shameful secret.

"You wouldn't go along with his rules if you

weren't positively gagging for it where he's concerned."

"*I am not!*"

But she'd been blushing furiously because, lord have mercy on her soul, she was. Ever since she'd understood what sex was, she'd wanted to have it with him. Who could blame her? He was far too sexy for an impressionable teenage girl to cast her eyes upon. And she could remember him coming over to her parents' estate in Upstate New York and swimming in their pool. In a tight black swimsuit that had left little to the imagination, and dear God, the man's chest.

She'd had her sexual awakening then and there. She'd become a *woman* that day.

Her friends in school had sighed over smooth-faced pop singers and she just couldn't understand the fuss. She'd found the man she wanted. She couldn't get excited over boys.

The wrenching pain and excitement she'd felt when the lawyer had told her she'd be going to live with him…

It had been like being trapped in a strange, gothic fantasy. Her parents were dead, the estate was being cleaned out, and she was being sent to live with the gorgeous, austere man of her dreams, who saw her only as a child.

Because she had been a child.

She was not one now, however.

She remembered her last conversation with Mariana about Apollo, as she'd tried so desperately to hide her reaction to Mariana even speaking his name, tried to preserve a shred of dignity.

"Dieu, Hannah. You're in love with your awful old guardian. What a cliché."

"He isn't old!"

"You follow his ridiculous rules because you're so into him that it's embarrassing. You glow while talking about how he won't let you go out. Like you're a child."

"I can go out!"

"Go out with me then. Dance with another man. Kiss another man."

It had echoed inside her. *Kiss another man.* She'd never kissed *one*.

Because she'd always wanted to kiss Apollo.

But she'd been the model, well-behaved ward. It didn't make him want her. It didn't make him love her. She had stopped believing he might when she was about twenty.

She could remember, viscerally, watching him come into the foyer of his sweeping Athens home, dressed in a perfectly cut tuxedo, and her heart had just…nearly exploded. She'd been on summer holiday and returning to stay with him was always a mixed bag. One part agony, one ecstasy.

The cliché of it all.

Then a woman in red had come through the front door. His age. Sophisticated, in her thirties, speaking with him effortlessly.

They'd gone out together arm in arm and she'd understood. It would never be that way between them. She would always be a child to him and he would always be a stratospheric object she wouldn't be able to touch.

That didn't mean she stopped having sex dreams about him, that didn't mean her feelings for him were gone. It was why being around him was still so painful. At least with the agony there had been ecstasy when she'd been able to imagine he might want her back someday. After that, she'd been left with only agony, and as long as she was in proximity to him, as long as he remained in control of her life, it wouldn't stop.

The violent negative reaction she'd had to the idea of kissing another man had been her wake-up call. No matter what she told herself, she was still in love with Apollo. And that needed to stop.

So she'd gone out with Mariana. She'd tried to find another man to kiss, but when it came down to it, she hadn't wanted to kiss anyone.

Then when she'd gotten home just past midnight, he'd told her coolly that she wasn't to do that anymore. No anger, of course. He acted as if she was a wayward child who'd made a mistake.

She'd sat on the edge of her bed with the world caving in around her.

She loved him.

He saw her as a child.

The arrangement wasn't fair or normal.

It was holding her back. *He* was holding her back.

She'd said as much to Mariana the next day at work.

"You have to get him to release you from the guardianship!"

"I don't think I can."

"Sure, you can. Drive him to the brink! Make him wash his hands of you."

She didn't want Apollo to wash his hands of her. No matter the twisted-up feelings in her chest, no matter that she needed to get rid of some of them, he was her only real...family. He meant the world to her. He would never be nothing to her. But he couldn't be everything like this. She had to be able to breathe. To be herself.

She needed to have the control of her life, of

her money, of her work, so that he didn't have all the power.

She'd told people he was easy. Permissive, even. He wasn't. It was only that she'd never once gone against him because she was so horrifically infatuated with him that she'd let herself be his cheerful little doormat. She hated that for her.

It was like, through the eyes of Mariana and the rest of her friends, she'd gotten a good, hard look at her life for the first time, and she could feel all her certainty, all that she'd ever believed about herself, unraveling.

She was alone. He'd taken care of her, but he'd never offered her anything…emotional, and she was so enraptured with him it was like the sun shone out his billion-dollar butt.

She accepted far, far too little from the people she gave love to.

Another problem.

Questioning things with Apollo made her go back further, it made her question things with her parents. The parents she could hardly remember—not because they'd died six years ago—but because they'd never really been around when they were alive.

They'd loved her. She assumed. Because parents loved their children in theory. An innate instinct that kept them from drowning you when you were too annoying, she'd heard.

They hadn't been cruel. But she'd never been as important as whatever adventure they wanted to take, or business venture they'd wanted to embark on. She'd been lonely as their child, she'd been lonely as an orphan.

Because no matter how much she loved the people around her, they didn't show it back.

And she felt...stuck now. Trapped in the consequences of her parents' actions, their decision to make Apollo her guardian in case they died. Their decision to bind her in the most patriarchal nonsensical trust fund situation she could imagine.

Under Apollo's care until well after she was an adult. Unless she was under a husband's care. And it did say, *husband*. Otherwise, she'd be tempted to ask Mariana to marry her and offer her friend a kickback for doing her a favor.

She wanted to be free of this. Of him.

What she didn't expect was to see...there was more than just anger in his eyes now. This was something else. There was heat there, and she was no expert on the goings-on between men and women, but she was pretty expert on Apollo and his expressions, his movements. There was a fire in his eyes like she hadn't seen before.

And danger.

She sensed danger.

But it wasn't the kind of danger that she wanted to run from. No, it was a predator's gaze. Watchful. Waiting. Hungry. It didn't frighten her, because it mirrored the feelings she'd carried for him for all of these years.

Her breath exited her body in a rush.

He…wanted her.

Or at least for a moment, he had looked and seen her as a woman.

It's working.

No, that's not what she was doing! She didn't want him to be attracted to her, she just wanted to get out from under his authority so she could go on and be a functional, human adult who wasn't hanging on his every move.

She couldn't deny that this moment, being pinned beneath his dark gaze, was the single most erotic moment of her life. It was like everything had stopped around her, yet her body had come alive. Her heart was pounding, a mirrored pulse beating between her legs. Her breasts felt heavy, her knees shaky.

She wanted…

She wanted to go to him. She wanted to touch him. She wanted…

And then, as quickly as that heat had flared in his eyes, it was gone.

If you want him to wash his hands of you, follow your teenage dreams and seduce him like an idiot. Do you really think a virgin's inexpert fumblings are going to make him abandon the Apollo of it all?

No. Apollo was a locked box filled with nothing but honor. If she dared disturb that lock, she would disrupt everything.

She couldn't afford that.

She'd made friends at her new job, and she loved them. But in the grand fabric of her life, there was one thread woven all the way through.

Him.

This was a very dangerous high-wire act she was doing. Trying to get him to be frustrated enough to let her have her freedom, trying to get him to understand she was too old to be treated like a child.

Then there was the matter of her father's company.

It was being taken care of by a Board of Trustees. Because, yet again, it was another thing that technically belonged to her but could not be hers until she was twenty-five. Or married.

She thought of her friends at the hotel she worked at. Of all the things that she could do for them. If she owned an entire hotel chain, she could give Mariana the hotel to manage. God knew she was better than the frosty manager where they worked. She had ideas. Energy.

And the idea of something belonging to her… That excited her.

The foundation would always belong to her father. But she didn't hate her father, even if she was newly going over some of her resentment.

What she needed was to get her own life.

What she needed was to not be in love with Apollo.

And that brought her right back to the moment.

His burning gaze made her feel as if the flames there had reached out and licked over her skin. Though the fire now was much more apparently anger.

"I think working at this hotel is not good for you. Your friends there are a bad influence on you."

Then her rage matched his own. How dare he?

"You can't tell me where to work, Apollo."

"I am your guardian," he said.

"And I'm an adult. Not a child. But you have failed to notice this."

"The stipulations of the guardianship indicate that your father would not have considered you a full adult until you were twenty-five."

She had kept her emotions locked down for so long. Kept herself in check. And for what? He would never look at her and see why she had done it. He would never understand how much she had loved him. In that way, he was the same as her father. The sharp hook of emotion that curled around her gut at that thought left her gasping.

Was this how it would always be? Her loving men who didn't have the time of day for her? Was she such a cliché that her daddy issues were manifesting like this? She was just so overwhelmed. By shame. By anger. At herself. At Apollo.

"My father wouldn't know," she said, the words wrenched from deep within her. "He didn't spend any time with me. At sixteen, I did a competent job managing my own life because I had to. Because my parents were ever off on adventures. They got themselves killed in a canoeing accident, for God's sake. It isn't that there's... There's nothing wrong with going off and having adventures, but they did it instead of caring for me. That things became more heavy-handed after their deaths just seemed all a bit wrong to me.

"You're not in charge of me," she said. "Not really. I might not have access to my trust fund, but I have a job. I have friends. I don't need you intervening in my life."

"Sadly for you, *agape*, you do."

"No, I don't."

"You do. Because should I decide to withdraw my support from you, your trust is locked for a further five years."

"What?"

"That is the way of it. If I decide that your behavior is immature and unwarranted, I can hold your money up for five years."

"And what if I marry?"

"If you marry, then your husband is…"

"*My guardian*?" she spat. "You can't be serious."

Yes, her whole life was supposed to be this. Authoritative men telling her what to do, building her little gilded cages. Never, ever loving her the way she wanted them to.

"I am your guardian, exactly. And yes, I am serious. But do not take your rage out on me. I did not create the stipulations of the agreement."

"You're threatening to enforce them."

"For your own good. Your father entrusted you to me. I have done an excellent job with you."

"You have done *nothing*," she said. "You have laid down a series of arcane rules and regulations, and I followed them because I was nothing more than a doe-eyed child where you were concerned for years and years. But I am not that girl anymore. I am a woman. You cannot tell me what to do."

"I can and I will. Go to bed. Go to your work shift tomorrow and give them your notice. Then come straight home afterward."

"I won't." And that was when she decided she would make him unreasonable. She would make him prove himself a liar because he wouldn't do it. Shortly. He wouldn't push it, so he was her guardian until she was thirty. Not even Apollo would go that far. There was no point to it. But then, she couldn't understand why he was being so unreasonable now.

"I will do what I think is best," she said.

"You know nothing of the world," he said. "That is why your father put me in charge. He was very aware that he had raised a little princess who knew nothing beyond the walls of your gilded cage, and he would no longer be here to protect you. He put me in charge because I know what's beyond the gold and glitter, *agape*. And you do not."

He knew it was a cage. He just didn't care. His use of the word she'd just thought herself made her even angrier. It was difficult for her to hang on to what the goal was right now, not when she just felt…rage. At all the years of being so lonely, so unseen, so unloved.

"He put you in charge because he was a *misogynist*. If he had a son, he would never have done that."

"You're a daughter. The world is not a kind place for women. Surely you know that."

"He might have had some confidence that I was smart enough to avoid—"

"Regardless of gender, avoiding victimization is not a matter of being smart. Believe me. I know."

There was something in his eyes then, something different even than the heat that had been there a moment before. It was a weakness. And it stopped her short.

She had never seen anything half so human in him before. But much like the heat before, it was gone before she could truly grapple with what it meant.

There was no point arguing with him anyway. Apollo was a man who understood action. Not words. She would show him that he could not bend her to his will.

And then part of her wondered…

Wondered if the heat that she had seen in his eyes would make him bend. Would make him withdraw.

He wasn't immune to her body.

Even if he had hidden it quickly. Even if it had only been momentary.

She was going to have to ponder that. What it meant, and how she could use it.

The idea made her heart start beating faster again. It was a risk. For all the reasons she'd thought of already, it was a risk. It could push him away forever. But it could also be the thing that made him realize that now he needed to distance her—just for a time.

Or maybe…

Maybe he would give in.

For one moment she let herself imagine that. His lips, his hands, his body.

She had never tried manipulating anyone ever in her whole life. But the idea that she might be able to make him want her like she'd wanted him…it sent a shock wave through her system.

Get a hold of yourself.

One thing was certain, she couldn't control Apollo. But she could control herself.

She wouldn't be told what to do.

So, she turned on her heel in his office, and when her back was to him and she was near the door, she stopped. "You're not my dad."

Then she swept out of the study.

CHAPTER TWO

"YOU'RE NOT MY DAD!" Mariana laughed uproariously as Hannah recounted the scene in Apollo's office.

"Well," she said, unsure if she was being laughed at in praise or...because she was silly. "He isn't."

"Going to skip the very obvious joke here," their friend Pablo said, leaning back in his chair and grinning. He was wickedly handsome and very gay—a boon for her visually, but nothing more.

"Appreciated," said Hannah. They were sitting in the back of the club, the light swirling around them. Because Mariana worked as the concierge, she got them the best access to the very best places, and that usually at a discount. Because, after all, she had to have experience so that she could recommend things to guests.

They were sitting around a white table, enjoying some delicious champagne, and finally, she had told them everything that happened last night.

"You should get married," Rocco said. He was Italian. Very attractive. *Not* gay. She wished that she could muster up some enthusiasm for Rocco. Of course, it probably wasn't a great idea to date someone you worked with.

"I did think of that," she said. She looked at Mariana. "Actually, I would marry you," she said.

"I'd marry you too," Mariana said, tilting back her champagne glass and swallowing the rest of it down. "I would literally be marrying my best friend."

"Well, the will says something about a husband specifically."

"How narrow-minded," Mariana said, frowning.

"It may shock you to learn that my white billionaire father wasn't exactly known for his expansive take on the world."

Gigi, the bubbly redhead who was the newest to join their friend group, giggled. "A big shock. Though, it must have prepared you to work in customer service at a hotel."

"Mmm, possibly." Of course, none of their customers could ever hold a candle to Apollo. She had looked at him with rose-colored glasses for so long. And why? Because he was stunningly attractive? Because he was over six feet tall with broad shoulders, arresting features, a square jaw, a blade-straight nose, and lips that looked like they might soften if he smiled. But he never did, so it remained nothing but a theory?

This was her problem. She was a cliché. An absolute cliché. Hideously lousy for the older man who had stepped into her life as an authority figure. Which was problematic and unrealistic. Many would argue that she did not have the agency inherent in the situation to feed feelings like that. So there, stupid heart.

She had never interrogated her life before she'd gotten this job. She was just thankful that she had a group of friends who had encouraged her to do that.

"I googled him," Pablo said. He stole a cherry from her drink and popped it into his mouth.

"Who?"

"Apollo Agassi. Your stern daddy of a guardian. He's a snack."

"Oh, for God's sake," said Hannah.

"I'm just saying," said Pablo. "It's completely valid that you have a thing for him."

"I want to see," said Mariana, taking out her phone. "*Wow*. I'm so sorry I mocked you for wanting to bang him because— OMG."

"Right?" Pablo said.

They passed Mariana's phone around and gaped at the pictures of Apollo.

"He's hot," Gigi said.

"Wouldn't know," said Rocco.

"Yes," Mariana said. "You're straight. We know. Thank you."

"So, get on your knees for him and take control of the situation," said Pablo.

That image was instant, and graphic.

"I'm sorry, *what*?" Her cheeks felt like they'd been scorched.

"There's no way he hasn't noticed that you're an attractive woman."

"He thinks of me as a child," she said, but then she thought of how he had looked at her last night, and she wondered.

"He's a man. And men are simple. Get on your knees, do something better with your mouth than just talking back, and see what happens."

"*What?* You think he'll just… He can't give me access to my trust fund. He isn't legally in charge of that. He's just in charge of me. Kind of? I don't know. It's convoluted." She didn't even bother telling them that he could extend the length of time that she had to stay on the guardianship because it was just unhinged. "I can't just… Do *that*. It would…"

"What? What's the worst that could happen?" Mariana pressed.

Well. He could use that as an excuse to extend the time between now and when she got her money. But, most likely, knowing him, it would make him want to push her away. Apollo was exacting. He didn't expect people to do the unexpected, and it was one of the reasons that he had found her behavior over the last six months so challenging. She knew that. Nobody defied him. And it was why she was fighting him with such intensity tonight.

You wondered about this…

Yes, she had. But that meant like…wearing a low-cut top in front of him, not actually touching him. Tasting him.

She'd wanted a little plausible deniability with her behavior, and something like that would leave no room for her to pretend that maybe he'd imagined it all.

"If you want your freedom," Pablo said. "Take your freedom. In your mouth."

"*Ugh*," said Mariana, taking a cherry out of her drink and throwing it at him.

I'll think about it," she said, and it made her feel all warm and uncomfortable.

"Hannah is a virgin," Mariana said.

"*No*," Gigi and Pablo said at the same time.

"It's true. She's probably the only virgin in here."

"Really?" Rocco pressed. And he looked… Interested. She tried to figure out how she felt about that. She wished she could feel something about that. He *was* attractive. In a more conventional way than Apollo, who was arresting more than he was beautiful. Tall and imposing.

Rocco was in his early twenties. Smooth and pretty, even. Age appropriate, even. Imagine that. No undue power over her life, even.

She was instantly uninterested.

There was something broken inside of her. She was convinced of it.

"Yes, I am," she said. "Didn't I tell you that he's tyrannical?"

"The issue is that you don't know how to give a BJ," Pablo said.

She sniffed. "How hard could it be?"

Pablo lifted a brow. "It can be very hard, Hannah."

She laughed, in spite of herself.

"You can practice on Rocco," Gigi said, smiling.

Rocco lifted a brow. "I wouldn't be opposed."

It all felt a little bit dangerous. But this had been what she was after, right? Adulthood with no limits. She *could* practice on Rocco if she wanted to. She could do whatever she felt like.

"You should dance with me," said Rocco.

"The way to my heart and a…a—" she couldn't say it, so she cleared her throat imperiously "—is clearly not dance, Rocco, or I wouldn't be a virgin."

"No strings attached."

"Okay."

She took his hand, got up from the table, and let him lead her to the center of the dance floor. She wasn't tipsy. She had only taken a few sips of her drink, and if anything, she had more of a sugar high than a buzz from the alcohol.

Then he pulled her close, and she noted that his body was hard. That he was thoroughly built, even though he had a lean look about him. And she still didn't feel the stirrings of desire. Or anything close. It was blasted inconvenient.

And suddenly, a large masculine hand went to Rocco's shoulder and pulled him away.

Hannah started and looked up. And saw Apollo standing there, looking furious.

"What did I tell you?"

Rage, shock, need, and a feeling of being very small all poured through her. He was here. For her, but not in the way she might have wanted. He was here to scold her like she was a child, and it made her want to weep, wail, and yell at him. And she also wanted to fling herself into his arms. She wanted to take that conversation she'd just had with her friends and make it real.

She wanted that as much as she wanted to run.

She let anger drive her forward, because of all the emotions it felt clearest. Safest.

"What did I tell you?" She took a step toward him. "You are not in charge of me."

The anger she saw in his eyes was just as sharp as hers. It was exhilarating. Intoxicating. Making him respond.

But then he moved. "Let us see," he growled.

He bent down and picked her up, throwing her over his shoulder.

"Apollo!"

She looked around, expecting someone to come to her rescue at any moment because there was no way they were letting this brute carry her out of here bodily.

But nobody came to her defense. Not even her friends.

"Apollo," she shouted, kicking until her shoes came off, hitting his shoulder with her closed fists as they exited the club and made their way outside.

His hands were warm, his hold firm, and it was impossible to feel only anger when he was touching her like this. But it was all the same futile emotion that had had hold of her for all this time. She wanted him to touch her as a man touched a woman. He was touching her like an angry parent would carry a child. But that didn't make *her* feelings change.

"I own that club, *agape*," he said, his words hard.

"You do *not*," she said.

"Yes, I do. As of about ten minutes ago."

"You... You bought the club so that you could carry me out of the club?"

"Yes. All things considered, I think it was worth it."

"You're unhinged," she said. "You're a sociopath. *A psychopath*. Put me down." She wiggled against him, her breasts pressed against his back and sending sparks of arousal through her, even as she wanted to destroy him. Make him feel this same endless need. Make him suffer like she did.

"I am none of those things," he said. "If I were, I probably wouldn't be so angry. I would be looking at this with a cool sort of sophisticated calculation, and instead, I wish to dump you into the sea."

"*Good*. I would rather tangle with the sharks than deal with you."

"The sharks may end up being your only option."

It should terrify her, the idea of losing him. Right now, it didn't.

"*Great.* Find me chilling with the hammer-heads. But then you wouldn't be able to control my life, and what fun would that be for you?"

"I will not fail," he bit out.

He set her down on the sidewalk, the ground gritty and cool beneath her feet. "You are a foolish girl," he said. "I have been tasked with taking care of you. And I will do so. I will do exactly as your father asked me because he is one of the only people who ever did a damn thing for me and didn't expect something in return. With him, it wasn't transactional. And nothing else in my life has been that way. And I will honor that. I will do this with excellence as I have done everything else."

"I am *not a spreadsheet.*" She was made of feelings. Of desire and need and aching hunger, and he was turning her into a *thing*. It outraged her. "You can't math out the way that you handle this. And what metric would you even use? The successes that I achieve? And then, would any of them be mine?"

"A question you would always have had to ask yourself, as you come from money. As you would always be standing on the shoulders of your father. So, if that's going to give you an existential crisis, it would have anyway."

"I'm *not* having an existential crisis." Sadly she knew what her crisis was.

"Then what is all this?"

He looked at her, and then he looked her up and down, and she suddenly became very conscious of how her dress conformed to her curves. She had chosen the dress because it was provocative, but now beneath his gaze, she felt naked.

But she saw it then. The masculine appreciation in his gaze, even though he tried to bank it, tried to bury it and deny it. She could see all of it.

She thought of what Pablo had said.

The idea filled her with desire and need.

She hadn't felt any of that when she'd been dancing with Rocco. But the image of getting on her knees before him made her feel liquid. If he dragged her back to the car, she could do that. Slide to the floor, find herself between those powerful thighs, and undo his belt...

She wanted it. So bad. It made her heart throb painfully, and that secret place between her legs ached.

She wanted this man. Even now. She wanted him to tear the dress from her body. And she wanted to wrench the clothes from his. She wanted to have him while they fought. It was like a fever. An illness sweeping through her like a tide.

"What's the matter, *agape*? You look flushed."

How dare he? *How dare he* when he was not immune to this thing either.

"I think you know exactly what I'm thinking about."

"What is it exactly?" he asked.

She was suddenly aware that the street they had gone out to was an alley and deserted. The sidewalk between her feet suddenly felt warm rather than cold, as it had a few moments earlier.

The warm Grecian evening was suddenly hot.

And all of her plans had shifted. In the time since he'd carried her out of the club she'd realized this was more fraught, more perilous than she'd thought before. This was...the end of her sanity. He couldn't have all the power anymore.

She had to take some for herself.

She had to touch him.

She had to make him feel this. Understand it.

She had to.

She took a step toward him until her breasts touched his chest. She tried to suppress a shiver. Trembling.

"Perhaps you're angry with me because you

feel I haven't provided adequate compensation." Her voice shook, her heart beating so hard she felt it in her temples. "What if I showed you how appreciative I am of the work you've done for me?"

"You must be drunk," he said, not moving away, staring her down defiantly, his face like stone.

She would not be dismissed. She would not let him do that.

"I'm *not* drunk. I barely had two sips of my drink." She was high on something else. On her outrage. On the clarity she felt now. Understanding that she had power here. That he felt this too. And how desperate she was to force him to feel it. Really feel it. Like she did. "I know exactly what I want."

He stepped toward her, his dark eyes glinting. "And what is it you think you want, little girl?"

He didn't think she would follow through. He thought she would be afraid. She wasn't.

"I would really like to get down on my knees and show my appreciation. You would like that, wouldn't you? I can see that you're not immune to me. I've seen you looking at my body these last couple of nights. You like my dress, as much as you wish you could hate it. If you ask very nicely, perhaps I'll pull the top down and let you see—"

"*Enough*," he ground out, gripping her arms and pushing her back a step. Her eyes widened, fear and triumph warring within her. "You're being a fool. I'm your guardian. You are my ward; you are under my protection. A child."

"I'm twenty-two. I'm not a child."

"You might as well be one to me. I was friends with your father, I've never been friends with you."

"What does friendship have to do with desire? What does it have to do with—"

"Enough," he gritted out.

And she did it, she mustered every ounce of bravery she could and looked down, and she saw. That burgeoning hunger there, pushing against the front of his pants.

"You want me. Your body doesn't lie."

Calling on a boldness she had no idea she possessed, she reached her hand forward, and her fingertips brushed that jutting arousal.

His lip curled as he moved her hand aside. "You think that's significant?"

And suddenly, his face transformed. Pity and contempt were reflected in his gaze. But the need was still there. Regardless of what he said.

"You're hard," she said. "You want me."

"You silly little girl. That doesn't mean quite

so much as you would like it to. A man can get hard for anything. Sex is cheap. You have no idea how cheap. It means nothing to a man like me. I've had more lovers than I can readily count. More than I could ever count. Because I don't remember most of them. And why would I? I feel nothing for them. And you... You're young. You have a nice figure—soft skin. A man is bound to respond to you. But don't forget that a man would forget you as soon as he had you, darling. It is not a compliment to make a man hard. It is simply biology. It means nothing about how I feel for you."

"It means that you see me as—"

"It means *nothing*," he said again. "You are a silly child, and the fact that you think it signifies anything reveals your inexperience. No, spare me. Your tantrums and your paltry attempts at manipulation. That you think I would break all that I am for the chance to touch you is the most foolish thing I've ever conceived of. I can find someone to take care of this as soon as I get you locked up in the house."

She had thought he might react badly. She hadn't truly imagined this. His cruelty. The way he cut her with such unerring precision. Hit at everything she felt insecure about.

And it all boiled over.

"*I hate you*," she said. Then she meant it.

With every fiber of her being. As much as she had ever loved him.

"Good. Perhaps you should hate me."

He picked her up and carried her to the car then, and she felt scalded by his touch. Outraged. But she didn't wish to protest too much because she didn't want to rub her body against him. They were silent on the drive home, and then she went to her room and locked the door defiantly behind her. She took her phone out of her pocket and called Mariana to let her know she had gotten home safely. And what had happened.

"Rocco told us."

"A lot of good Rocco did."

"Well, you can't exactly blame him for not wanting to have a fistfight in the middle of the club."

It was true. It wasn't like he was her boyfriend or anything. Or her...

"Mariana, I have to call you back." She hung up. And then she dialed Rocco.

Her hands were shaking. And she was desperate. Desperate to get Apollo the way he'd gotten her.

"Thank God," he said. "I was worried."

"Rocco," she said. "I think you should marry me."

CHAPTER THREE

APOLLO SPENT THE next two weeks in a vile temper. He had taken his feral mood off to Scotland to see Cameron, business partner and friend, and his wife, Athena.

"Stop brooding," Cameron said one night. "You're doing a classic impression of me." He grinned, his scarred face shifting with the expression.

"My friend," Apollo said, "it is not an impersonation of you unless I lock myself away in a castle for more than a decade and make my business partner do every last one of the in-person appearances we have scheduled for the company for the duration."

"I am sorry about that," Cameron said.

Then he laughed. It was good to hear Cameron laugh. He had not done so for a long time before Athena came into his life. Truly, he and Cameron had never had much to laugh about. But his friend had always been gregarious and beautiful, so handsome that the people around him paid dearly for the chance to spend time in his company. And when they were younger, had paid astronomical sums for a night with him.

He had seemed unscathed by all of that until an accident killed his lover and stole his looks. And yes, during that time, he had been a veritable beast.

Apollo would love to claim the way he had handled Cameron as another of his good deeds, but he could not. Cameron was his brother. In all the ways that it mattered. They had come up together on the streets, and they had kept each other from dying. Apollo had spent the early part of his life in Greece with his mother, the bastard child of her affair with an Italian man who'd left before Apollo was born.

She had gone to Scotland on the promise that a man there might care for them, but it had turned out to be little more than human trafficking. His mother had lost herself during those years, and Apollo had run away from home.

It was too dangerous, being around his mother's various clients. He had managed to remain unmolested. Until that was, he had decided that charging money for access to his body before people could take it for free was perhaps the way forward.

It was the kind of work that took pieces of your soul. He and Cameron had not done it because they'd had a vast array of choices before them. They'd had certain assets and had used them how they could.

They were also brilliant. Smart with technology and had begun working at getting their hands on all the pieces of old technology that they could so that they could begin understanding the inner workings of all of it.

The ugly truth was that they had been prostitutes. The uglier truth was that sex was a commodity people paid dearly for. He did not feel guilt over his past actions. He had done what he needed to do. But it had changed him. When your own body was for sale, it forced you to live in your mind. He and Cameron had done so to their own benefit, and with connections they'd built—and some exploitation that verged on blackmail—they had managed to begin establishing themselves in the tech world. Starting their own company. Letting go of that old life.

Yes, he would love to say that staying connected to Cameron during his crisis, keeping him moving, keeping him going, had been an act of charity on his part. It wasn't.

He hadn't known how to live in a world without Cameron, and beyond that, his financial success was tied to Cameron. And he would not allow failure.

They were billionaires. They had more money than a single person could ever spend in a lifetime, but Apollo would never take that for granted. How could he?

The wolves of poverty ever snapped at his heels. The wounds never fully healing. He knew what he would do to survive. He did not have to wonder. He would do it again. But it would cost so much more now. Because, as a boy, he'd had no pride. As a man, he did. And therefore, failure was not an option. Not now. Not ever. He simply could not and would not allow it. But Cameron was healed now. Not because of Apollo, but because of Athena.

The woman who had stumbled upon his castle a few years back, running away from her own troubled past. Cameron had fallen in love with her, whatever that meant.

Apollo couldn't be certain.

He did not understand it. He knew what it was to be bonded to somebody because of flame and fire. He knew what it was to feel as if he owed someone a debt. As far as romantic love went, to him, it looked as if you simply chose a person you wished to have sex with for the rest of your life.

Apollo had never been the playboy that Cameron was.

The way that Cameron handled the trauma of their youth had been to shag everything that moved. Once he had money and power. Cameron was always taking delight in how his beauty caused those around him to do foolish things. It was why his accident had taken so very much from him. It had been the way he handled the world.

That face of his.

As for Apollo, he often felt fatigued by sex. The transactional nature of it. The way that it sometimes pushed him into a strange hollow cavern inside of himself. Where his body was moving but his mind was no longer there.

That was another difference between himself and Cameron. Cameron had never cared who he slept with. Other than his wife, who was now the only person he would ever want, he had gotten so much pleasure out of the act of being the desired object that age, gender, nothing, none of it mattered to Cameron.

An advantageous position to be in in a life such as theirs.

It did matter to Apollo. He'd had to do things he had not liked. With people he had not wanted, and he'd had to figure out how to manufacture a response to them.

It was difficult to break old habits. And that was why he found himself sometimes retreating during the act. All these years later. It didn't make sense to him. And it was frustrating, because he liked women. He liked sex. But it could never entirely be divorced from the way he had once used it, and that outraged him. Because he was a man who had defeated the systems of this world. A man who had climbed up from the gutter defied all odds, and in many ways, he had escaped.

And yet, a film clung to him, and he did not know how to clear it away.

And then of course, there was the matter of Hannah.

He was doing his best not to revisit that night.

The way that his body had responded to her, because what he'd said to her had been alive. It was true, arousal, desire, was cheap for many. And bought expensively. He knew that better than most.

But for him? He had eminent control over his own responses. Always. Whether he chose to react or chose not to.

But he had chosen nothing with her. When she had looked at him with that beautiful face, her lips parted, her expression earnest, and told him that she wished to get on her knees and thank him for what he had done…

The twist of self-loathing in his gut was intense.

She was offering him payment. He had wanted to take it.

It made him feel… Wrong. All of it was wrong.

He wanted to go back to the night before he'd first confronted her about going out. To before he'd seen her in that dress that had barely covered her body. He did not want to see her as a woman, but as a symbol of his redemption and he was outraged she had pushed things to this point.

As if you did not have a part in it, putting your hands on her body and carrying her out of the club?

He had refused her. That was what mattered.

He had prevailed.

"Are you going to tell me what the problem is?"

"No," said Apollo. "Because there is no problem, Cameron. The presence of a problem implies I'm concerned there is something that I cannot fix. We all know that can't be true. I don't lose."

"You didn't fix me," Cameron pointed out.

"I triaged you. Until your wife appeared."

Cameron laughed again. "You could not have arranged that if you'd tried."

Apollo leaned back in his chair, surveying his friend's castle. It was all a far cry from squatting in vacant buildings in Edinburgh. "When I move, the universe orients itself around me, or did you not know?"

"Your ego is doing well despite the rest of your mood."

He let silence reign for a moment.

"Hannah has become difficult." He shouldn't tell Cameron this. But Cameron was truly the only friend he had in this world.

"Oh, the adult woman whose life you're still in charge of? Imagine that." Cameron's amusement outraged him.

"I did not create the set of rules surrounding the guardianship," he said. "She acts as if I'm the enemy too. And I did not create the situation. I neither wrote the will nor got myself killed in a canoeing accident. That was her mother and father."

"I imagine it doesn't much signify when you are the object blocking her from the things that she wishes to do and have and be."

"I am doing nothing of the kind. I guided her. Through high school, through college. She has a degree, she could get any job she wished. She could get a job at her father's company, and then when the restrictions on her lift in three years she will take an executive position. She's going to be in control. It will be hers."

"Three years when you're in your twenties is an eternity. And after all these years of being under your iron fist."

Cameron had no right to comment. He hadn't been present for any of this. "I resent that. I have been fair. I have been good."

"Of course you have."

"Cameron, you are a pain in my ass."

"I have been for more than twenty years. Why stop now?"

"I do not know what to do with her."

"Give her what she wants. Give her the respect that she is due."

"I worry for her," he said. Because it was true. Though mostly, perhaps he worried that he wouldn't be able to keep his promise to her father, which would be unacceptable. A failure. And if he put his foot on that path, what then?

"Let her have her freedom. You can stick to the terms of the will, and you can make her happy."

"What makes her happy right now is going to clubs and dancing with strange men." The way he'd felt when he'd walked in and seen that man, with his hands on her, had made him feel a violent surge of possessiveness. It was, he told himself, because she deserved better.

That man transparently wished to use her for her body and Hannah deserved more.

The thought of her being used in that way made his lip curl. Made him think of the dark things behind him.

"She *is* twenty-two," Cameron pointed out. "There's nothing wrong with going out, dancing…having a bit of casual sex."

"You can say that after the life we led?"

"Apollo, for most people, this time of their life should be carefree. You and I know nothing about that. My dear Athena knows nothing about that. She was a prisoner, her father kept her from living the life that she truly wanted. Is that what you want to be for Hannah?"

"I am not like Athena's father. I did not kidnap Hannah from her rightful family and then attempt to sell her into marriage after hiding her away for her entire life."

"No of course not. But I'm only saying… There are normal lives to be had out there. Just because we didn't have them doesn't mean Hannah can't."

"But the world is…"

"Dangerous," Cameron said. "Horribly so. But you will be there. To protect her. If she truly needs it. Don't be a monster in the meantime. That really is stepping on my territory."

He pondered his friend's words, even as he went back to Greece.

He moved back to Greece after Cameron's accident because it had felt… It had felt like something he should try. An attempt at finding some of himself. He hadn't found it. At least he didn't think. There was no point going over the past. There was only moving forward. And he was intent on doing that with Hannah.

He arrived home, expecting to find the place turned inside out. Expecting that she would have thrown a party to get revenge on him.

He had left, knowing that she might act out in his absence, but he had felt like it was safer than remaining near her.

He had done what he had to.

But when he arrived home, not only was the house in order, Hannah was standing there in what was a perfectly demure outfit, one that should not have brought his blood to a low simmer and made his body feel set on edge.

"I'm very glad that you've arrived back home. Because I have something to tell you." She sounded placid. He didn't trust it.

Her hands were clasped in front of her, and just then, she moved. And he saw a large diamond on her left hand. "I'm engaged."

"You are *not*," he said, the words bordering on a growl.

Her expression was bland. "I am. You saw the man that I was dancing with at the club. Rocco. I'm marrying him."

That wee boy? That child? Who had pawed at her body as if it was a buffet platter he felt entitled to? Never. There had been no love on his face, no care of any kind.

Most unforgivable of all, he had let Apollo take her. Any man who surrendered a woman so easily did not deserve her in any capacity.

And any woman who had offered what Hannah had offered him could not truly want another.

"You're *marrying* him?" he asked. "When I took you off the dance floor, you offered to get on your knees and pleasure me not one minute after you were in his arms? How can you wish to marry him?"

"I'm in love with him."

No.

The denial was instant and vehement.

"You're in love with him, and yet you offered to take me in your mouth?"

It was a dangerous thing, bringing that up.

"Old fantasies die hard," she said, and the words sparked questions, a fire that tumbled along his skin, and he wanted to ignore all of the implications there.

He had to focus on the issue at hand.

"No. I forbid it. You are not getting married."

"Funnily enough, the guardianship agreement says nothing about you having a choice in who I marry, Apollo. You can't stop me. We are to wed in two days' time. At the small chapel at the hotel. I hope to see you there. But if you're too angry at being outmaneuvered to do so... Well."

"*Outmaneuvered.* You don't love him."

"I do," she said. "I am prepared to live with him as man and wife for a year. At least. As the will stipulates."

"This is foolish. And childish."

"You think me foolish and childish, and that is why it's what you see. You are not in charge of me or my life. I'm getting married. My trust fund will be mine. And so will my father's company."

"And it could all be his as well. Did you ever think of that? The will gives outrageous weight to the opinions of the person you married. It is set up so that your husband becomes your guardian. Are you that stupid that you would overlook that?"

His words were cruel, and he knew that. He also knew that they would not wound her. They would only make her angrier. But he himself was too angry to be calculated in the moment.

"I'll see you at the wedding. Or I won't."

"It has to be a legitimate wedding. Overseen by the board of—"

"I'm aware. I went over everything with a fine tooth comb. I've known Rocco for eight months. We are in a relationship. We are in love. People have seen us together many times. We have passed our interviews with flying colors, and everyone is invited to the affair. Including you. Even though I hate you."

Rage was a roiling, ugly monster in his gut. He had not felt this sort of anger in many, many years. That she was the source of it made him… he was not trustworthy right now.

"You have not begun to hate me, Hannah," he bit out. "That is a promise."

But Hannah was not cowed. This was not the biddable girl who had been in his care all those years. Not the still, clear reflection of his own goodness that he'd seen as she'd done well in school, worked hard, presented herself with such care.

This was a woman. The one that had ignited his desire so unexpectedly even as she had called up his rage. This woman was on a path of destruction, and he could see in the reckless light in her eyes that she knew it. And was willing to let herself be destroyed if she could claim even a momentary victory.

"You will not best me, Apollo. That is my own promise to you."

With that, she left him standing there in the entry of his magnificent home, the evidence of all his billions soaring around them in the form of clever architecture, high arches and priceless artwork. Feeling as if he had no more power than he did when he was a boy.

But that feeling lasted only a moment. Because it was unacceptable. Because he would not indulge it. Because he would not allow it. He would not be manipulated by a child.

He would see an end to this. One way or the other.

CHAPTER FOUR

SHE HAD DONE IT. She had put the plan together flawlessly, and now it was her wedding day.

The chapel was in a beautiful location, on a rock that overlooked the brilliant jewel-bright sea. It was a white building with a blue domed roof and glittering windows. Her wedding dress was a beautiful liquid silk gown that shimmered as she moved, little crystals covering all of it.

The minute the wedding had been scheduled she'd been given access to her trust fund to pay for the affair.

It meant that she and all her friends were outfitted splendidly. And if she had slipped in a few purchases to make her friends' lives better and filed them under wedding expenses, so be it.

She needed this. And she knew she had likely compromised her relationship with Apollo forever but...

She couldn't go on like this. The night he'd carried her out of the club had made it clear. She was lost to him. Willing to debase herself, even as he humiliated her. When it came to him she wasn't rational or reasonable. When it came to him she made terrible choices that could not be endured.

The only power her father had given her was this. She had to use a man to escape another one, and while she hated it with every fiber of her being, she knew it was the only thing to be done.

Apollo had vanished after that night at the club.

Part of her had hoped he would storm in and apologize. That they would find some other way forward, but he hadn't come to her. He'd left town. Hell, he'd left the country. And so she'd moved forward with her plan to get away from him on her own terms.

She hated it. But she needed it.

She couldn't see past the next three years. If she sank deeper into her obsession with Apollo, there would be nothing left of her.

She had to do something.

This was the only something she could think of.

She gathered her bouquet, a stunning coral arrangement with bright blue blossoms sprinkled throughout that matched the blues around them, and looked at Mariana. "This is the right thing to do, yes?"

"Of course it is," said Mariana. "You're getting your freedom. And listen, I can't… You have been extremely generous. Thank you."

"I'm going to get you a job at my father's company. My company."

"You know this is not why I became your friend," said Mariana.

"No, I know," she said. "But I think you're great at your job, and I think you'll bring something to the company. And I understand that… It's not really fair that I've been given all of this. Yes, I have the education to do all of this, but very few people could simply step into this position. Especially not at this stage. I'm not owed any of it. But I do want to have freedom. Agency. I feel like I deserve to at least manage the assets that I was left, even if I'm not entitled to them."

Because the truth was, she could walk away without doing this. She could get a job, be just like her friends. Her anger prevented that. Her anger at her father, at Apollo.

And even more so, doing that wouldn't have the effect on Apollo that this would. She needed him to feel her anger. To feel her defiance. And only this would do.

"It's all right," said Mariana. "You don't have to justify yourself to me."

"Maybe I'm trying to justify myself to me. Because I'm doing a kind of extreme thing to get out of dealing with Apollo for the next three years of my life."

"That's okay. The whole situation is unusual. Could anybody really blame you?"

"I guess not."

"What kinds of agreements do you have in place," Marianne asked. "To protect you?"

"What do you mean?"

"Rocco..."

"He's your friend. He's our friend."

"He is," said Mariana. I've known him for three years. I like him. But... Sometimes... Sometimes he says things that worry me a bit. And I... I would just hate for you to get hurt doing any of this. You could always marry Pablo."

"I can't just substitute a groom at the last minute. And anyway, it's a little bit too well documented that Pablo is not interested in women. And I can't have the marriage looking fake. It has to be legitimate."

"Yes. I get that."

Granted, nobody seemed half as concerned with controlling her life, and what she did than Apollo was.

"What do you think he'll do?"

"It's a lot of money," Mariana said. "And you're being really generous with it. I worry he's going to let that kind of thing go to his head. I'm not going to lie to you, Hannah, it's... It's kind of intoxicating. To have a friend who can suddenly open all these doors for you. But I can't control you, and neither can Pablo or Gigi. Rocco... He's going to be your husband, and I just worry that he's going to start to think he could make a lot of money divorcing you and taking things from you."

"I just..."

"The stipulations of your will didn't allow for prenup, did they?"

"But he and I talked about it and..."

"Yes, you have an agreement with him. But will he stick to it, or will he exploit you as a husband?"

"It's too late to worry about that," she said. "It just is."

Except she was now suddenly worried that she was taking her foot out of one bear trap only to stick it in another.

And Apollo's words echoed in her ears. That she was young and foolish and knew nothing of the world.

Remembering that, the way he saw her...

Apollo was the bigger risk.

She didn't like to think she was naive. She knew that people could take advantage of you. But she supposed that there was an element of naivete in believing that money might not change somebody. Maybe that was the kind of thing someone who'd always had a certain amount of access to money could comfort themselves with. Money was inevitable for her. And she had never had control of it, but she had also never felt the lack of it.

She was worrying about that even as she slipped on her shoes and followed Mariana to the main part of the chapel.

She linked arms with Pablo and walked into the sanctuary. And Hannah waited. Waited until the music shifted. Until it was time for her to walk down the aisle.

She had no father with her to give her away. And suddenly she felt extremely sad. It was a funny thing, grief like this. Tinged so often now with anger, and yet there was still so much regret. She could go days without thinking of her parents. Weeks. And then suddenly it just wouldn't make any sense to her that they were gone. Not at all.

Right now, though, was one of those times when she was shocked, almost, that they weren't here. For her wedding.

She had never let herself think about that.

Perhaps because she had never been in a space where she had really thought about having a wedding.

The whole Apollo tying up so many of her emotions had prevented her from dreaming about that.

She looked up at the white stucco ceiling. "I wish you were here, Dad. But if you were here, this wouldn't be happening." A tear slid down her cheek. Of all the absurd things. She dashed it away and continued into the sanctuary. Rocco was standing there, looking handsome and familiar. And most importantly, like her friend. She tried to push away the doubts that Mariana had just introduced to her. She didn't need to be filled with doubt.

She arrived at the head of the aisle and had just turned to take his hand when suddenly a man in a dark suit melted from the shadows behind him and turned.

Apollo.

Her heart leapt into her throat, thundering like a wild, trapped creature. His eyes were on Hannah, and only Hannah. He never paused to look at Rocco. He never looked at the crowd, at the priest.

His dark eyes burned into hers with intent, and she knew she had lost. She didn't know how. She didn't know what form it would take. But she knew, beyond words, that he had come to claim victory here, and that no one would stop Apollo Agassi from getting what he wanted.

"Step aside," he said to Rocco.

Rocco turned and looked at him, his expression one of fear. "I said step aside," said Apollo. "You will not be marrying Hannah today."

The words were like a gut punch. She stepped forward, and was about to tell him off.

"Yes," Rocco said, his voice shaking just slightly. "I am."

Well, he'd tried.

"You're not," Apollo said. "You have two choices. I either expose your true identity to all the people here, and call the police, and have you extradited back to Italy, where I think you will find a not very warm welcome waiting for you, or you take the payoff I'm offering, and I will not tell you how much it is. But it is better than prison."

Hannah could only stare, a cold feeling taking root in her stomach and spreading outward, rivaling the heat she'd felt a moment before.

She had been duped. And because of that Apollo was winning.

Her own naivete had hung her, just not in the way she'd imagined it might.

"I don't…" Rocco looked between Hannah

and Apollo. Hannah could only stare, shock winding through her.

"What is this?" she asked, feeling sad, defeated.

"I'm sorry," Rocco said.

"I…"

Apollo shoved him aside and came to stand across from her, right in his place. And it was as if Rocco had never been there at all. "You know, Hannah, I considered picking you up and carrying you off down the aisle. But that seems like a bit too much melodrama, don't you think? I think perhaps I could save everyone time by moving into my rightful place. Here. As your groom."

"What?"

"Oh, yes. Your plans have changed. You're marrying me."

It had not taken much for Apollo to dig up dirt on Rocco Marinelli. Or as he was known previously, Rocco Fiore, of Rome, who had a stack of petty misdemeanors that he had committed, minor cons and identity theft. And when the heat had gotten too much, he left Italy and came to Greece, changing his identity and taking a job at the hotel. Where, by all accounts, he had been a good employee, and a good friend.

It was entirely possible the bully had truly reformed himself. Or perhaps not.

Apollo trusted no one.

But even if the other man had reformed himself, it did not matter. He was going to see this through. If Hannah needed access to her trust fund so badly, if she wanted to assume her position at her father's company, she could do so, but it would be under his supervision for this next year. This was the best way forward. Cameron had told him not to intervene, but it didn't matter what Cameron said. This made the most sense. He would have to live with her as man and wife in that time, and of course, he would not touch her. He would continue to act as her guardian. Continue to guide her, continue to protect her. To fulfill his promise.

He would not lose hold of her, of this. He had come to that conclusion this morning, and it had driven him to this point.

"I..."

"He can't do this, can he?"

She turned toward the audience, toward the men on the board, and then back to the priest. "He can't," she said.

When she looked back at him, her eyes widened.

He turned to look behind him and saw that Rocco had fled.

"Well, you're without your original groom."

"This is irregular," one of the board members said from the front row.

"I love Hannah," Apollo said. He was very good at manufacturing words of love. The truth was, everyone should be horrified that he had rolled up to confess his long-hidden love for the girl he had been caring for all these years, but they wouldn't be. They would all think it was a boon for her because he was a billionaire, and because her father had trusted him, so what else mattered?

This was the truth of the world. There was nothing Apollo could do about it, except use it to his own advantage.

What they didn't know was that she'd offered to get down on her knees before him in the street, and that he'd been tempted…

No. Not tempted. A physical response was not real temptation. He would never have done it.

"You do not love me," she whispered.

"Little fool," he said, his voice a hushed rasp. "If you marry me, you will have access to your trust fund and the control of the company. If you don't, things go back to the way they were, and I can opt to have your time under my control extended. So, what will you choose, Hannah?"

He could see her calculating. She already knew she'd lost, but she had to be sure there was no other choice. He respected that even if he did not have the patience for it.

He saw as the defiance in her eyes was replaced with weary acceptance.

Good. He was inevitable. The sooner she accepted that, the better.

"Fine," she said, her cheeks turning red with anger. "I'll marry you."

"There now. That was not a difficult choice, was it?"

She looked as if she would cheerfully eviscerate him with her teeth at the first opportunity, but her happiness in the moment was not his primary concern. His concern was her safety.

And his own reputation.

"Let us proceed," he said.

He took her hands in his and felt that they were damp.

Her fingertips were cold.

Reflexively he smoothed his thumb over her knuckles, and her eyes met his again, confusion in those blue depths.

He took a moment to take a visual tour of her features. Wide blue eyes, a delicately upturned nose, full lips, a defiant, pointed chin. Her dark brown hair was styled in the waves that fell down her back, and her dress conformed lovingly to her figure. She was well curved, which was exactly how he liked his women. And she smelled like... Peaches and sunshine. Which was unlike anything he had ever thought he might want to draw nearer to. And yet with her, he found he did.

The words didn't matter.

They both repeated them.

They were lies.

And yet he would never forget the slight shift of her bare shoulder. The way the sun came through the windows and ignited a halo of gold around the edges of her hair. The shimmer of her dress when she shifted her hips and the silk moved like a tide over her body.

And the smell. Those peaches. That was what he would remember. Always.

There were few memories that he felt the urge to try and capture. Hold on to it. And the ones he did have were mercenary. He liked to think of when he had made his first substantial sum of money and had been able to turn down a regular client wanting to meet up for a quick shag. He remembered that because it had made him feel powerful.

He could remember the first time he walked into a party filled with rich beautiful people and made conversation with a woman who was exactly to his taste. He had taken her to his bed, because he had chosen to. Though it had not been the escape, the heady rush of pleasure he'd hoped it to be. He had done it, though. He had chosen it.

They were grim things. Defiant things.

They were not soft and lovely. Not sunshine and peaches and silk.

This he could cling to, not because it felt like a victory, but because it filled him. Every one of his senses, like all the natural wonders around them.

And then came the moment that he had perhaps forgotten for a reason.

"You may now kiss your bride."

Had they married in private, they would not have done so, but they were doing it here in front of the board, and he had professed to love her.

It was no matter. Physical touch could mean very little to him.

And yet the memory of how he had responded to her body two weeks ago lingered within him.

She looked panicked, and he gripped her chin, studying her. "I'm your husband," he said.

She did not relax beneath his touch. He leaned forward, and pressed his mouth to hers, keeping it brief and nearly chaste. And still, the crack of flame that woke within him was like nothing he had experienced before.

He felt her lips go pliant beneath his. Felt that resistance change. So that her mouth clung to his.

Everything was softness. Everything was peaches.

He pulled away.

And then that moment passed, and the ceremony was done. And he let the lingering impression of peaches slip away.

They turned to face the crowd, and the priest announced them. It was silent in the room. Everyone was staring with wide eyes. Uncertain of what they had just witnessed.

They walked down the aisle together, hand in hand. When they returned to the antechamber, he released his hold on her. "Go and speak to your friends," he said.

"But…"

"I assume we have an entire reception to get through?"

"I…"

"We are married, *agape*. Try to look as if you might be happy about it."

"I'm not. I was doing this to get rid of you."

"You had no idea that Rocco was a con artist, did you?"

"No. Was he trying to… Was he trying to

con me?" She looked genuinely hurt by that. And he felt the urge just then to soften what he had just said.

For many years he had dealt with her by paying for her life. And with that money he provided safety, structure. She'd had a place to stay when she'd been on holiday. But he'd not had to...contend with her. With her emotions.

It had to change now.

"I have no evidence of that. Only what he did in the past. He was clean as long as he was here. But... Given his inclinations, I would not necessarily want to trust him with a fortune of your magnitude. Or with... Or with you, Hannah. I fear he could've hurt you. I hope for your sake you did not really love him."

"And if I do? If I do love him, you are happy to have separated me from him?"

"If you loved him, then I am extremely happy to have made sure you won't have your heart broken by him."

"That's almost nice. Except you took the whole situation and manipulated it to your own advantage. All of the protections that you're concerned I don't have... Well, now you have access to the company. To all of my money."

The accusation that he was using her for money scraped close to wounded bone, and he found himself snarling in response to it.

"How dare you? I do not need your money. Nor your father's company. I am a self-made man. The company that I built with Cameron is the one that I want, and the one that I care about. But you are my responsibility. And now for the next year I will be able to guide you on this journey."

He'd only just purposed to be more gentle and here he was growling.

She's strong. She's not a girl. If she wishes to be treated as a woman, as an adult, then she will have to deal with your anger when she ignites it.

"You're asking me to trust you when you didn't think that I was capable of figuring out whether or not I could trust Rocco."

"Yes. I do expect that you might have a bit more trust for the man who has cared for you since you were sixteen years old than for the man that you met a few months ago."

"You didn't spend all those days with me. It isn't as if you raised me. Perhaps both you and my parents needed to take real stock of how much you had to do with the way that I was succeeding. I'm sorry, Apollo, but that is the truth. My parents were off on their adventures, and I was at home studying. I was the one choosing to succeed. You put down your rules, but I chose to follow them. We didn't even live in the same country most of the time. I managed my life while I was away at boarding school, while I was away at university. I am the one whose life was completely uprooted, and I am the one who had to cope with it. You weren't there for me emotionally. You think that because you kept me from ending up in an alleyway doing black tar heroin that you've succeeded in some fashion, but you do not recognize that I was the one who was there for myself. And now, because you couldn't stand some other man stepping into your position you... Physically removed him from his."

"If a man is marrying a woman, and it is possible to physically remove him, and marry her in his stead, he didn't truly wish to be there. Even if he did, he did not deserve to be. Had someone tried to usurp my place as your groom I would've killed them. I don't think I'm being hyperbolic."

The conviction in his words shocked even him. The darkness there.

Murder was one of the few sins he hadn't committed. And yet he knew without certainty he would do it if he had to.

She was his. His responsibility. He would be damned if anyone hurt her now.

"You're a bit of a monster."

"I never claimed I wasn't. You're the one

good thing I have ever done, *agape*. I will see it through to the end."

"And I don't have a choice in it?"

"Think carefully about that. Because the truth is you will have more choices now than you ever have. Do not squander it because you're angry at me."

It was then that her friend came through the door of the church. "Hannah…"

"Go and speak to your friends."

And Hannah obeyed, going off with her friend and leaving him there. Nothing would change. This wasn't a real wedding. And it would not become one.

It would be a marriage in name only for a year to protect Hannah and her assets.

He had made the right choice.

Like he always did.

CHAPTER FIVE

"WHAT THE HELL was that?"

"I don't know," Hannah said, her heart still beating wildly, disbelief rolling through her like a freight train.

"He just married you."

"Yeah, I know," she said. "I was there."

Her lips burned; her body burned.

The kiss had been short and chaste and nothing much to get excited about, and yet her nipples were still tight and sensitive, and that place between her legs throbbed. Perhaps it was the memory of what happened between them two weeks ago in the alley. Or rather what hadn't happened.

But either way, the kiss had affected her far more than it should have. But then, how was she supposed to remain unaffected in these circumstances? She had orchestrated this entire thing to get away from Apollo, and now she was his wife.

His wife.

She had dreamed of this.

But never quite in this fashion.

It was like someone had handed her a beautiful snow globe, then smashed it on the ground. All the glass, snow, and the little village still there, but…mangled beyond belief.

And she felt like the broken shards of glass were digging into her now.

"His wife!" she shouted out loud.

"Well," Mariana said. "I suppose that takes us full circle. Because you know, he's not your dad."

"It's not funny." She was maybe *dying*.

"It's kind of funny. I mean, he ended up having to marry you. And he was so furious about the whole thing. You know, when you offered to get down on your knees and—"

"Yes, I remember that. Thank you. I was there."

"Well," Mariana said. "Now he married you. So… Does this mean that you get to have a wedding night?"

Heat burned through her. "I am certain that would be a very bad idea."

"Why? It would probably be really fun. He is so hot."

"I'm aware that he is so hot. That's the problem. But the bigger problem is that he's… He doesn't have any feelings. At least, not the feelings that aren't anger. Every so often, I think maybe he cares about me and that's why he is so intense about protecting me, but I just think it has to do with his relationship with my dad. They were good friends. And it matters to him a lot that my dad trusted him to care for me. He's like psychotically intense about it. But really, that is the only discernible feeling the man has. Otherwise, he's… Unknowable. He doesn't seem to attach much to anyone or anything. He has his friends, his business partner, and he seems to care for them. But… He never has girlfriends."

He'd hinted at dark issues in his past, and knowing him and the degree to which he was locked down emotionally she wouldn't be surprised if there was some terrible trauma he'd endured. But he didn't share that sort of thing with her, because he didn't see her as a person.

She was a good deed he was doing,

She was already feeling shattered. Sleeping with him could destroy her.

But he isn't immune to you…

"Well, men like him don't. They're far too sophisticated for that. But then they have wives, and…"

"You don't suppose they're faithful to them, do you?"

"Of course not. I work at a hotel. The things that I've seen… And a lot of them involve infidelity. Even while wife goes out shopping for a couple of hours. So, no. I don't think men like that are faithful. But you're not in love with him. Not anymore. I mean, you have a little bit of an infatuation with him, but if you were to sleep with him, it would get it out of your system."

All of that sounded logical. Except she *was* in love with him. But she couldn't bring herself to say that now.

"All that sounds very worldly and sophisticated, but I'm afraid that I'm not that. Especially when it comes to him. I just get tangled up. I think he meant too much to me for too long, and it muddies everything. Because I don't know that I could without… Without having feelings for him."

"You said yourself he doesn't have any feelings. So, why can't that be the same for you?"

"You've done that, just had sex with people and not have any feelings about it?"

Mariana shrugged. "I have feelings about it. If it was especially good, I often wish that he would call. I'm not *un*feeling. And it's difficult when you have a physical connection with somebody, but they didn't feel the same, or it wasn't strong enough for them to want to reach out to you. But you just get over it."

She frowned. "I don't know that I want it to be a thing I just get over. That's the problem. I had to just get over so many things. I don't think I've ever had a lasting connection in my life. Apollo is really the only one. And that's kind of sad."

"Well. Listen, I'm glad that he intervened. Because as much as I don't want to think Rocco was deliberately going to scam you…"

She groaned. "Yes, I know. The facts can't be ignored there."

"Anyway. You're going to be okay, right?" Mariana touched her arm, the gesture of concern touching. She wasn't alone.

Things had felt fraught for a while now. And as important as Apollo was to her, and had been, it was good to know she wasn't alone anymore.

"Yes." She took a breath, determined to weather this without being watery about it. "Hey, I'm still in charge of my money, and the company. So, the offer still stands. I would like for you to manage one of the hotels. Anywhere you want."

"Anywhere?"

"Yes. I've been looking at the way that things are run, and the company has stagnated in the last few years. I think there need to be some top to bottom changeups in leadership. And I feel comfortable saying that you could be exactly what it needs. So yeah. Anywhere you want."

Mariana looked shocked. "I'll look at the catalog and get back to you."

"Good. I just want… You've been a big part of making me see what I needed to do to take control of my own life. And I really appreciate it. I want to pay back."

Mariana smiled. "That is really lovely. But you know, the thing about friendship is that you don't have to."

"I know. I just want to."

And that was her last good feeling for the next several hours. Because after that she was forced to parade herself through the most awkward reception anyone could've ever had, where they ended up skipping cutting the cake, and leaving early.

When she was shut into the limousine that she had arranged for herself and Rocco, with an unsmiling Apollo sitting to her left, she let her head fall back against the seat. "Now what?"

She tried to ignore his closeness. The heat coming off his body. All of it mixing with what Mariana had said to her earlier.

Get it out of your system…

"We go back home. We must live together, and we will do so here. It is the easiest thing."

"We just… Go home? We just act like that didn't happen?"

"No. I'm not suggesting that at all. Of course it will be like it happened. You will now take your position at your father's company. Your day-to-day is going to change drastically. And I will be here to offer support."

"But we won't go on a honeymoon or…"

He looked at her, his dark eyes unreadable.

"I wouldn't think so," he said.

"How come you don't have to make it look legitimate to the board."

"Because I'm me," he said.

"That's not fair. They're just letting you do it because… Because what? Oh," she said. "Because secretly they would rather like it if you were in charge. And that's what they think is happening. They think that you are having a hostile takeover."

"Probably."

"That is horrendously insulting."

"It is. But it is not what I'm doing. You have total control of your father's company. I'm not trying to take anything from you."

"Well, what a boon for me," she said. "Misogyny and classicism are really powering this whole thing."

"Everybody does what they think will be the most advantageous for them," he said. "We all do it. Your friend Rocco was doing it. It seems to me that he had a hard life in Rome. It also seems to me that he might've been trying to make something new for himself."

"You were willing to threaten that."

"Yet again, *agape*. Everyone does what they must. I do not judge anyone for it. But neither will I let them simply get away with it. Not if my needs are different."

"That is a very cynical way of looking at the world."

"Has any part of your life given you a different perspective?"

She shook her head. "No."

"I'm not a cynic. But I have lived. I had lived more life by the time I was your age than you would possibly believe. I had no optimism left in me about people."

"What happened to you?"

Because she had seen it. A kind of hollow desolate sadness in his eyes that she couldn't quite pin down. But she had never asked about his life. She had thought earlier that he had never shared, that he didn't see her as a person. Did she see him as one? For all her feelings about him, had she ever asked him about his life? What his experiences were before she'd known him?

No. Because she'd been so young when she'd met him she'd imagined he existed the moment he'd first appeared in her life and not a minute before. And even as she'd grown older she hadn't challenged that.

"Don't worry yourself about what happened to me. It is the kind of thing you don't want to infect your own thoughts. You did not have to live through it, and therefore you should not have to live with those images in your mind."

"You make it sound terrible," she said softly.

"I survived it. So perhaps it is of no consequence. I survived it, so perhaps it does not matter much if it was terrible. It made me wise. It is why I work so hard to protect you. I trust no one, because I know that every single person on this planet has an end to their altruism. A point at which they must see to their own needs, their own success. I do not judge them for it, but that doesn't mean I'll allow it."

"That's what you're doing with me. You think that what you want, your own success when it comes to your concept of seeing me through to adulthood is more important than what I want."

"Yes," he said. "I do. Mostly because I think

you want the exact same thing when you are able to understand."

"You really don't give me a lot of credit, do you?"

"Again, I have no reason to. You've been through some difficult things. But that doesn't mean you truly understand the ways of the world. As I said to you before. The world is not kind to women. Your father knew that. It is one of the things that he and I were both very aware of. The seedy underbelly of things. He had concerns for you. And the reason he made me your guardian was that he thought I was... Realistic. That he thought I would be able to protect you in a very particular kind of way. Because of what I had seen. Because of what I knew."

"What did my father know about anything outside of his privileged existence?"

"Do you know anything about your mother's family? Surely you must realize that if things were functional in your family there would've been a network of relatives to take you in rather than your father's billionaire friend in his thirties."

"What are you saying?"

"The circumstances your parents came from are perhaps different than you were led to believe. And that is why your father prized my protection of you so much. Your mother and I endured similar things."

"And you're still not going to tell me what that is."

"No."

"Thank God you're not actually my husband."

"I am actually your husband," he said. "It was made legal only a few hours ago."

At that moment, the limousine pulled up to his house. Fury was like a living thing inside of her. He was doing nothing to shed light on anything in the situation, and she felt as if everything had been turned upside down, while he was intent on acting like it was all the same. It wasn't. How could it be? The man she had been in love with for so much of her life had married her today.

And all of her truths converging into one sharp point inside of her. The emotions so big it made her feel like the child she desperately didn't want him to see her as.

The realization her own father had put her in this situation was so painful she couldn't breathe around it. The horrible truth she'd let all this go on for too long because of her own impossible feelings.

Oh, no, she really was going to cry. The car

pulled up and she fiddled with her seat belt, frustrated that it wasn't simply coming undone.

She was coming undone.

She hated this.

She hated him.

Maybe as much as she had ever loved him. Except one feeling hadn't shifted the other to the side like she had thought it would. No. It was all just painful.

Because for her this was the twisted perversion of a dream she had never even allowed herself to have, and for him, this was all just a victory. Proof that he was supreme. Proof that he was in control. Emotionally, it didn't touch him. The only thing that had ever come close was when she had challenged him sexually. That he had responded to. That had sent him to Scotland. That was when she had realized she had power.

So perhaps there was something to think about in Mariana's words. But she stood by what she had said. It might be too costly for her. And that was what scared her. Because right now she felt as if she had been skinned and rolled in salt. Right now, she felt like all of the most vulnerable things about her had been brought dangerously close to the surface, and a slight breeze would create a ripple large enough to reveal all.

So, she escaped the car, went inside, and went straight to her room. Where she wrenched her wedding dress off through sobs.

She was married. She was married to Apollo Agassi. And yet wanting that to mean something was as impossible as wishing her father had been there to walk her down the aisle. Because her father was dead. And Apollo's emotions were just as remote, hidden beyond the veil that she could never reach. And neither could he. It was why she had sought to free herself from all of this. But by God, how she had failed. Spectacularly.

And then she stopped suddenly. Her dress was a pool of liquid silk around her feet, and the only thing she still had left on was the white lace underwear she had put beneath the dress. They were so thin they were barely there. The fabric for the gown was so delicate that barely anything could sit under it without being visible. The underwear had been astronomically expensive. Delicate like a web. Her nipples were visible through the cups, and the shadow of curls between her thighs evident. She examined herself in the mirror. She was acting exactly like her father and Apollo would expect her to act. She was acting like a child. When Apollo took control from her she allowed him to do it. It was not her. She was better than that.

Stronger than that. If she wanted to be treated as an adult then she had to seize everything she wanted. What would Apollo do, after all? What would her father have done?

They would have taken everything. Not a portion of what they wanted. She was so worried about her own emotions, rather than taking charge and committing to handling them herself. Apollo had taken control today when he had stepped into Rocco's place. But who would take the control now?

She slipped her high heels back on. And she examined herself in the full-length mirror. She didn't look like herself. She looked like a siren. Her legs were impossibly long with the help of the heels, the way they elevated her posture making her breasts look even more prominent. She was soft. She preferred a lazy day of reading to an afternoon at the gym, but she enjoyed taking walks around the city. And she felt the balance gave her a more pleasing figure than she had previously given herself credit for. But then, she had never truly looked at her body while considering showing it to a man.

What would he see when he looked at her? She had seen need in his eyes when he'd looked at her before. Remembering it now made her heart race.

She might ruin everything. But wasn't everything already ruined? A smashed snow globe. A mockery of her past fantasies.

But her need for him wasn't mangled in all the wreckage. It was as bright and clear as it had ever been.

She wanted to be consumed by him.

He had married her today. Wrested control from her. Taken her own plans and burned them to the ground.

But she could have this.

She was past the point of considering. She was doing it. Her father had been a leader. And she was now going to lead that company. He had clearly doubted her ability to do so. But this was her moment, and she was going to own it.

She took a breath, and opened the door. He did not have staff in the house at this hour, which meant it was only the two of them in the manor now. She also knew exactly where she would find him. In his study. If he was so convinced that things were going to stay the same between them, then his routine would remain the same. It was just like him. To be just so. It was like him, to go right in for a little bit of evening work.

She paused, her heart pounding so hard she couldn't hear anything but the insistent rhythm. This could destroy everything.

Oh, Hannah. It's already destroyed.

That sad, internal truth made her want to weep.

But she wouldn't weep.

She wasn't a child.

She was a woman.

She was going to show him.

She pushed the door open. He didn't turn. Of course, he was certain that she had come to yell at him. To castigate him. He wasn't even interested.

"Apollo," she said.

"I'm working, Hannah."

"I believe we have something to discuss."

He turned, and immediately, the fire left his eyes.

"There is the small matter of our wedding night."

CHAPTER SIX

SHE SLOWLY CROSSED the room, and rounded the other side of his desk, sitting on his lap. He made no move to stop her, didn't lift his hands to touch her, nor did he push her away. He was warm and hard beneath her. And she was trembling, but doing her best not to show it.

"I want my wedding night."

"Hannah," he said, his teeth gritted. "Stop."

"You act like I don't know what I'm asking for. But I do. I'm twenty-two years old. I know exactly what I want. You have denied me my groom. Will you also deny me a night of passion?"

"You don't get to ask that of me."

"Why not? It seems like it would be an appropriate thing for a married couple."

"We are not a married couple. Not in that way."

"But I want it," she said. "I want to please you. I want to please myself."

He reached up, unexpectedly, and gripped the back of her hair, his hold tight. He forced her head back, tilting her chin up. "And what is it you hope to gain from this? Are you playing with me?"

"No," she gasped. "I'm not playing with you. I want you."

"Is it a *thank you* that you wish to give? Paying me back for my help? Do you thank all the men in your life that way?"

She tried to shake her head, but he held her fast.

"I don't," she said.

His eyes were like obsidian. Dark and without end.

"Stand up," he said, releasing his hold on her hair.

"But I…"

"Stand up. Take your clothes off. Show me what's mine."

She hadn't expected that. And she wondered if he was trying to call her bluff. If he was trying to prove that she would be too frightened to do what he asked.

This was not the guardian who had set boundaries for her these past years. This was not the man who had taken care of her, or even the one who had stormed the altar today as a method of protecting her.

This was a different side of Apollo. One she had not seen before. She had caught a glimpse of it that night at the club, but it was as if she'd been looking through a cracked window. She had the impression of it but no more.

This was *more*. It was everything.

And so was he.

So she stood, ignoring the thundering of her heartbeat, and unhooked that bra, before pushing her panties down her hips and letting them fall to the floor. She stepped out of them, remaining in her high heels.

"Turn."

She did, in a full circle, letting him see her body, her skin burning beneath his gaze.

"You have been pushing me these past months."

She nodded. "Yes. I have been."

"And you think you know what is out there? You think you know that you can handle all of this. You know what waits for you. You know what men want. Come here."

She obeyed again.

He beckoned her with his finger, and she found herself sinking down to the floor, on her knees before him, between his spread thighs. A version of what she had fantasized about that night that he had carried her out of the club.

He bent his head down, gripping her hair

and pulling her head back, tilting her face up toward him. Then he leaned down and pressed a hot, open-mouthed kiss to her throat.

She gasped. And he captured her lips with his, swallowing down the sound of surprise as he slid his tongue against hers.

She was shaking. Trembling.

His lips were magic, his tongue wicked as he licked deep into her mouth, claiming her. Changing her.

Forever she would think of this. This dark room. The smell of woodsmoke, and the flavor of whiskey, and Apollo.

This would be her wedding night, forever etched into her memories. Not gauze and romance or whatever else a girl might imagine she would get on her wedding night.

But this dark, hot thing that burned between them like a living ember.

He was angry. He did not kiss her out of a sense of passion, but as a punishment. And she was too weak to deny it.

He was giving her what she wanted, but only in part. He was holding himself back, forcing her to swallow his anger down if she wanted any of his desire.

And she did. So she took it. All of it.

When he pulled away from her she was shaking. She could see that he was aroused, and he moved his hands to his belt.

She pressed her knees together, her body liquid.

"Let's see how well you can attend to this task. And then I will tell you whether or not you have earned your wedding night."

"I don't understand."

He unbuttoned his pants, and slid the zipper down, freeing his arousal. It was beautiful. Long and thick and more glorious than she had imagined it could be. She was obsessed with him. His body. His scent. His strength. Even now when he was being cruel she desired him.

There was something about it that called to her. That took all the things that they were, all they had ever been and refashioned it so that it was finally all that she had desired. Because she had spent much of her life with him as her guardian. Giving orders and commands and setting out boundaries. And in the midst of all that she had idolized him. Desired him. Wanted to be the focus of his attention, of his desire. And now she was. All of the things he had ever been to her, all the things she had ever wanted, converging at this moment. Well no. That wasn't entirely true. There was no softness here. Not even a little. Not one bit.

"If you please me with your mouth, then

I might give you what you want." He said it again, his voice authoritative. And it made her shiver.

"You like control, don't you?" she asked, looking up at him from her position on the floor.

"Control is everything, *agape*. Without it, what is a man? He is a slave to those around him. And I will never be that."

"Of course not," she said.

She wondered what was beneath those words. He had hinted at his past, but he had not gone into detail about it. So she still did not know exactly what haunted him.

But she could see that he was haunted now. There was something feral in his eyes. And she felt herself responding to it. She wanted to quiet it. To give him whatever he needed to banish those ghosts.

She had set out to do this to please herself, but she realized pleasing him would always be part of that. It was inescapable.

Tentatively, she leaned in, wrapping her fingers around his thick shaft, and then she flicked her tongue out, tasting him.

Desire was a living thing inside of her. She parted her lips and took him inside her mouth. She had never even kissed a man until tonight. This was in many ways going fast. Except, it didn't feel like it. Because even though it had been a formless, nameless thing within her, she had desired him all this time.

He was every fantasy she'd ever had, and the task of being asked to fulfill something for him was so intoxicating she was on fire with it. She looked up, and met his gaze as she swallowed him down. And the strain on his handsome features was everything she needed.

How much she wanted this man. Always. She was desperate for him. Obsessed with him. It was like she had opened the door on it now and everything was laid there before her.

Her need. Her desire. The truth of it all.

Everything. She would have everything.

She continued to lavish attention on him with her lips, her tongue, and he growled, grabbing her hair again.

"Slow down," he said.

"I can't," she said.

"You will. Use your tongue."

She obeyed, licking him from base to tip and back again before taking him in deep.

He made a rough, masculine sound and let his head fall back against the back of the chair.

She reveled in it. In the obvious evidence that he was undone by this. That it wasn't only her.

This was equal ground. Perhaps the first equal ground he had ever stood on, with her on her knees and him above her, his body exposed, his pleasure being guided by her own mouth.

She had never fully appreciated how it could be. The way sex could strip away the layers, could twist and upend the power differentials between them. He was powerful in this, of course he was. Strong and authoritative, the one with experience. But she had power as well. She was the one who had come in without her clothes on. She was the one who made him tremble even now as she lavished attention upon his glorious body.

She was the master of this moment, even as he, rough and strong, revealed his own weaknesses through the way he chose to dominate.

She could feel when she was getting too close when he physically pulled her back. She could sense when he needed to exert himself because she had scraped him too near the bone.

She did not feel young. She did not feel inexperienced. She was nothing more than stardust. Shimmering with need. Beyond age or time.

It didn't matter who had come before. In his case, probably more lovers than she wanted to know about.

And in her case none. But it was as if everything melted away. As if the world had gone to nothing outside of this warm, dim space.

The fire roared. His breath was harsh and jagged, her own heart beating loudly in her ears, her sounds of enjoyment resonating through her as she tasted him.

And then he moved her away from him.

"That is enough."

"You didn't come, she pointed out.

"I know," he said. "But you wanted sex, didn't you?"

"I thought I had to earn it."

"You have," he said, his tone rough, jagged. It cut into her. The realization that he did not surrender to this need between them easily. That even though he wanted her, he didn't want to want her.

It was written all over his face, the stark lines tracing the edges of agony, ecstasy, all at the same time.

But her heart beat with certainty. I want him. I want him. I want him. Every beat, every breath.

It all spoke to the same need.

"It's your turn to sit," he said.

He stood, and she dutifully took her place in the chair that he had just occupied.

He stood two feet away from her, his eyes hooded, unreadable in the firelight.

"Spread your legs," he commanded. And she

found herself parting her thighs and ignoring the embarrassment that washed through her.

He began to unbutton his shirt, undo the cuffs. He consigned the shirt and jacket to the top of his desk, before moving slowly to remove his pants and shoes the rest of the way.

He stood naked before her, and she could barely breathe. He was a glory, with the flames dancing over those hardened muscles. The hollows exaggerated by the absence of light. His shoulders were broad, and so was his chest, well defined with dark hair sprinkled across it. His stomach muscles were prominent, hard. There was no excess fat on his body at all. His hips were lean, and his masculinity hung heavy between his legs. Still hard. Aroused.

Because of her. His thighs were thick, and the strangest thing of all was how intimate it felt to see him without his shoes and socks. His bare feet were somehow an intimacy she had not counted on.

This was Apollo. The man she had known all these years, for she had known him long before he had ever become her guardian. Her father's close friend and confidant. The man who had taken care of her, even if imperfectly all these years.

The man who was giving her what she had

demanded of him, even now. Even as it seemed to separate his skin from his bones.

Never was there a moment so suspended in time. One that reached deep within her and seemed to grab her heart, stopping it. It throbbed against the squeeze, making every breath a battle.

Apollo.

She had wanted him all these years. But she had not truly understood what that would mean.

But there he was now, naked and raw, and she could taste him on her tongue. It was no longer a theoretical fantasy. It was happening now.

She had never thought sex would be so uncomfortable. As it was glorious. But her need verged on pain, and she was certain if someone were to touch her skin they would find it feverish.

Her hair was damp where it rested at the back of her neck, and she was not sure whether she wanted to run away from him or run to him. So she sat, legs spread, as vulnerable to him as he had been to her just moments ago.

The look on his face was that of a predator. Sharp and intent.

He moved his hands down to his heavy shaft and curved his fingers around it, stroking himself lazily as he looked at her. She had to look away. Her face was hot, embarrassment rolling through her.

"Look at me," he commanded. She did so without another thought.

"If you're far too embarrassed to see the way that you affect me, then you are too embarrassed to take me."

"I'm not," she said.

Terror streaked through her. Would he deny her even now? As far as they had gone, would he stop this? Would he make her leave? Humiliate her?

Perhaps that's what this was about. Him exerting his control. Perhaps it had all been a lie from the beginning. This idea that they were equal because they were naked. No. She felt so vulnerable then. As if her obvious need for him was written all over her body, and the pleading expression in her eyes, and the obvious slick heat between her legs.

"You must be certain this is what you want. And this is not a payment," he bit out. "When I sink into you it will be because I want to. And it had better be because you wanted to."

Did he want it? Did he want her?

"You will owe me nothing in the aftermath, and I will owe nothing to you. This is not a transaction."

His words were fierce and feral, and she

didn't know where they came from, but it was somewhere deep within him. Guttural and fearsome and real. They reached down deep and soothed a wounded place within her, but she felt like she was looking at his scars. At his own pain, and she wished she could make herself fully understand it. Wished she could understand him.

"I hear you," she said.

"Do you? You need to not look upon me with shame. Look at me." He moved his hand over his shaft more times. Swift, decisive.

"This is what you do to me. On that. This is what it does to me to see you naked like this, sitting in that chair with your legs spread wide. If that makes one of us a monster then it's me. But I am far too old and far too jaded to let that stop me. You have pushed me to this point. I know you must accept the consequences. This is your last chance."

"I want you," she said.

"But do you want everything that comes with that?"

"I don't know what that means."

"There is no way to know until this is finished. Are you willing to accept the potential consequences of that?"

"Yes," she said.

"Good. Good, one leg over the arm of the

chair, then the other." She did so, the move leaving her even wider open to his examination.

He went back to his desk and opened the drawer, taking a box out. Condoms. It made her scalp prickle. Knowing he had condoms in his desk drawer. In his study. Did he have women here often? It was an uncomfortable realization.

You should tell him that you're a virgin.

She didn't want to. Because it felt like making herself even more vulnerable, and she didn't think that was fair. Already she was the one sitting here legs spread wide. Why did he deserve more? He wouldn't tell her about his past. He wouldn't tell her about the women that had come before her, who had perhaps sat in this very chair. Why should he hear about the lack of lovers in her life?

She did not need to be known by him if he would not allow himself to be known by her.

So she shoved down that desire to share. That desire to find some closeness with him, because that was simply an illusion. They would never have closeness.

He was not promising love. The consequences he spoke of were not a life together.

And she was okay with that. She was.

She had fantasized about him loving her when she'd been younger. When she hadn't understood that a man like him wasn't built for love, marriage, and a family. She knew better now. It hadn't killed her feelings for him, but she did know better.

One thing she knew now with clarity was she could never have handled this before.

This was far too raw. Much deeper, much more feral than she'd imagined it could be.

It was glorious.

And they were glorious.

But it would not end anywhere beautiful.

It would end in ashes. It would end in tears.

Those were the consequences that she was willing to accept. To have him. To feel him moving inside of her.

Instead of putting the condom on, he moved to her again, dropping to his knees in front of her. His face was scant inches from the most intimate part of her and she found herself squirming beneath his close examination. She wanted to run. She wanted to get away.

But she didn't. She held fast. Because he was right. If this embarrassed her, then what was the point of it? It only proved that she wasn't ready. She was not half so worldly as she imagined herself to be.

She would not have that.

He moved his hands beneath her body, cupping her rear, lifting her up from the seat as he laved her with the flat of his tongue. She gasped, her hands going to the back of his head.

And he began to taste her deeply, exploring her, finding every drop of her wetness and taking it for his own.

She gasped as he pushed a finger inside of her, and then another.

He didn't need to hold her up anymore, because she was arching up in the seat, unable to stay still as he licked and sucked her.

Until she was trembling. Until she was crying out. Begging for release.

He moved his fingers quickly, before sucking that sensitized bundle of nerves at the apex of her thighs deep, and she shattered.

"Apollo," she gasped, tugging at his hair as she cried out his name, cried out her release. She felt spent. Shaken.

She was trembling.

He moved up, sucking one nipple into his mouth, and palming her other breast, sliding his thumb over the distended tip there. And then he moved to her mouth, kissed her deeply, letting her taste the evidence of her own desire on his tongue.

He kissed her. And it didn't end. It went on and on, sending new ripples through her as he traced shapes on her tongue with the tip of his.

And she found another climax rising up inside of her. Not quite as intense as the last, but present all the same, her internal muscles rippling as the unexpected orgasm overtook her. Just from his kiss.

From the carnality of what they had just done.

She was limp against the chair, and that was when he moved away from her, took the condom packet, and tore it open, rolling the latex over his thick shaft slowly.

She whispered something. A curse, maybe. Encouragement, perhaps. She couldn't be sure. She was lost in a haze. Her whole world reduced to this. To him. To the desire that burned between them.

"Please," she whispered as he pressed the head of his shaft to the entrance of her body.

She wanted him. So much. He gripped her hips and pulled her forward, impaling her on his glorious length. She gasped. In pleasure then in pain. There was a slight tearing sensation, yes, and it did hurt. But it was over quickly enough.

She rolled her hips against his, instincts driving her now. And if he had been about to pause, if he had been about to say something, he wasn't now.

He began to move, canting his hips forward, thrusting deep within her.

So deep that she could hardly tell where he ended and she began. This was sex. And she wanted it to be making love, at least a small part of her did. She thought of what Mariana had said. That sometimes, when it was very good, you simply couldn't help wishing it could be more, no matter what you thought when you went into it.

But you got over it. Mariana had gotten over it, and Hannah would too. This was a rite of passage. She was living a fantasy. She had broken this powerful man, she had made him abandon his principles. For the chance to be with her. It inflamed her. Ignited a need inside of her. It made her feel strong and powerful and like more than she had ever been.

Today was her victory. What he had tried to take and make his own she had reclaimed.

And she would accept the consequences of that. She would not allow herself to cry. Not at the beauty of what was passing between them now, not at the intensity of it. Not at the deep unexpected nature of what it meant to have someone inside of her.

No. This was her victory. Her pleasure.

And she would have it all.

He gripped her hair again, and she tilted her head back willingly as he kissed her neck, down to her breasts, thrusting in time with each kiss.

Then he took her mouth, murmuring filthy promises against her lips that set her on fire.

Her skin was damp all over, the heat from the fire and their own created need all slick and intense.

Her heart was pounding so hard it was as if she had run a race, and she was not done.

He spoke in Greek. English. She had always loved to hear him talk. His accent wholly unique and *his*. Cultured because he had trained it to be, but retaining hints of Greece and Scotland. She liked it even more when he spoke these words over her. When he lavished praise upon her body.

When he gave her everything.

Everything.

No. Not everything.

Just sex.

But that thought did nothing to temper her desire, and finally, she broke. Her orgasm igniting her anew, taking her to new heights as her internal muscles squeezed him tight, drawing a response from him.

He growled, his thrusts becoming faster and faster, losing their rhythm as his own climax overtook him, the unraveling swift and certain, his cry of release a growl, that mingled with her own. She clung to him even as he began to ease away from her.

"There," he said. "You've had your wedding night."

"That… That's it?"

She was still lying on the chair, spent and limp, uncertain of what to do or say.

"It is what you said you wanted."

"Apollo…"

"Did I promise you more?"

Tears pricked her eyes. "No. You didn't. I'll… I'll go back to my room."

"Please," he said.

And she didn't bother to collect her underwear. Why would she? Her dignity was in tatters, and pausing to collect clothes would not restore it.

She held it together until she got back to her room. And then, she broke.

CHAPTER SEVEN

APOLLO STOOD AT his desk, his hands planted firmly on the high-gloss surface. He looked down at the floor. There was a pair of white panties and a white bra, evidence of what had just happened, and if it was not there, he might've thought it was a dream. If not for the spent condom in the wastebasket, if not for the fact that his heart rate refused to come down.

If not for the fact that he felt guilt. Deep, dark guilt that was unlike anything he had experienced for some time.

He had felt used before. It was part and parcel to the life he had led prior to becoming what he was now.

But he had always been very careful never to use a lover. It was possible he'd used her here.

Or that she had used him.

A wall had come down during this and he… he had no defense against it. He had never felt sex in quite this way before.

He had been cruel to her.

He had wanted to punish her for pushing him to the brink, but had that all been justification for being with her? She was beautiful. But why did that matter so much? There were many beautiful women, and they were not in his care.

How had he been so weak with the one woman he should never have touched?

He was reeling. Reeling from the intensity of it all. From the way it had torn down the walls within him.

And he could see them all. Every man, every woman that had paid to use his services, knowing that he was desperate. Knowing that he was poor. Using their power and privilege to gain access to him.

Their faces melted with his own in his mind. Hannah had said she wanted him, yes, but he was the one with experience. He was the one who knew about sex.

She had taken to everything they'd done with enthusiasm, enough that it was easy to convince himself that she had perhaps more experience than he had thought.

He was caught between two sets of beliefs in this moment.

That he had used her, or that she had used him.

That she'd had a few lovers, and that she had been a virgin.

He had felt resistance when he thrust into her. But she barely reacted to it. She certainly hadn't seemed to be in pain.

So perhaps he was wrong. It was entirely possible.

She had gone down on him like a champion, and that made him suspect she knew her way around a man's body.

But perhaps that was just convenient thinking. And maybe it didn't matter either way. Because it wasn't truly about her, what she had or hadn't done, but about whether or not he had taken advantage of the situation they found themselves in.

She came to you.

She had. But he had created the situation.

And she used you because she was supposed to marry someone else...

He poured himself a measure of whiskey and sat down in the chair where he had just taken her.

It could not happen again. She would start her new position at her father's business next week, and he would be on hand to make sure everything went well. Things did not have to change. They could go back to the way they were. It only made sense.

She did not need a lover. She needed guidance.

And there was no reason to think things had to change.

He was resolved. He owed her his service, and he would do everything he needed to do to arrange his schedule so that he could be there for her as she embarked on the next chapter of her life.

He would take the steps needed to continue to act as her guardian. Not her husband.

But she was his wife.

He stared at the white underwear.

She was his wife. And he had taken her on their wedding night.

His bride in white…

No. Just thinking those words opened up a strange cavern inside of him, and it was one that he wished to keep covered.

He had never entertained the idea of getting married. Had never thought that he might have children, or a family of any kind. There were certain legacies that seemed best burned to the ground. The earth salted.

He was happy for Cameron, but Cameron had always navigated the life they'd had differently.

For Cameron, the biggest trauma had been the accident. Of course, through it, Cameron had definitely become a kinder person.

Apollo was fine with his friend's arrogance, but there was definitely less of that now that he had fallen in love with Athena. He was more caring. That made him ache too.

But there was no reason to think along those lines. He was who he was. He had been created from a very specific set of circumstances and there was no use mourning what might've been.

If his mother had not been such a fool over men. She had found a way to stand on her own feet.

If she had not been so easily tricked.

If he had not been so hungry. If he could've found a way to exist modestly then perhaps he would not have thrown himself into the life that he had.

But there was no use regretting it. It changed nothing. There was a version of his life, perhaps, where he got an honest job at a shop and lived quietly in Scotland. When he married and had children. Where his childhood was a sad, regrettable footnote, and not a Hydra that had grown trauma on top of trauma and sprouted many heads.

He had not taken that path. He had taken this path. And because of that, he knew he could not have all things. Money, power, and normality. He had seared his own soul to the point he no longer easily recognized right from wrong. If he did, he would never have done this to Hannah.

All of it. From the wedding today to what had followed. To the aftermath of their passion.

He knew that she had consented. His concern was that she hadn't been entirely aware of what she was consenting to.

And that was not something he had reasoned through in his lust clouded mind.

How could he be half so basic after living the life he had? Hadn't he had enough damn sex?

Had she thought of someone else the whole time? Used his body as a surrogate for what she really wanted?

Dieu. What did that matter? He was the one who was supposed to care for her, and he didn't like these echoes of his own shame, of his past, rattling around inside him.

He poured another drink. Because tomorrow he was going to have to face this head-on. And tonight he didn't wish to think about it at all.

He needed his walls firmly back in place.

When Hannah woke she was sore. That place between her legs was tender, and her skin felt hypersensitive.

She grimaced as she sat up, the memories of the night before coming in hot and fast.

That hadn't been a dream. She knew it hadn't

been, because there was no way she could have conjured up any of those images in her mind without actually having experienced them.

Her imagination just wasn't that good.

She lay back down and rolled over, burying her face in her pillow as she groaned.

She was… Humiliated. She had acted a perfect slut for his enjoyment. And then he had sent her away. Was it because he was embarrassed by how much she had wanted him? By how she had acted?

She rolled back onto her back and kicked her feet. Then she pulled her blankets over her face and took two breaths.

Okay. She pushed the blankets down. She was going to deal with this. She was going to deal with herself. She wasn't a coward. She was about to be the CEO of a major company. She was married to one of the most powerful men in the world. They were married.

That was a whole thing. The whole thing she really wasn't sure how to handle.

"Deal with it. Get a grip. He's probably not even here." Still, when she dressed, it was in a turtleneck and a pair of slacks. It was not flattering, but it covered up a lot of her body. And she just couldn't handle how exposed she felt. It seemed like the best way forward.

She made her way downstairs and then

stopped when she smelled coffee. And heard movement.

Was he really still here?

She took the last few steps at a trudge, and then she entered the kitchen. And there he was. Wearing a low-slung pair of pants, his chest bare.

It was a stark contrast to the way that she had sought to cover her own shame.

How nice for him.

"Good morning," he said.

He turned to the espresso machine and began the process of making her drink with what felt to her like an overdramatic dedication to deliberateness.

Not that an espresso wasn't appreciated at any time, but at the moment, she felt like maybe they had something to discuss. Recent experience had taught her Apollo would not instigate. She would have to push.

"Is it?"

"You know, I have never fully understood—and this could be because English is my second language—whether *good morning* was a statement about the fact the morning was a good one, or if it was a wish that the other person have a *good morning*."

"I couldn't say. Nor do I think it's entirely relevant to our present situation."

"Which is?" he asked.

"Well. There's the fact that we got married."

"Yes. And that has changed things. I assume you will be headed to the corporate offices today," he said.

"Not today. They're in New York."

He lifted a brow. "Oh, I'm well aware of where they are."

She scoffed. "I don't have a plane ticket."

"You do have free use of the private jet," he said, waving his hand. "Your father's. Or mine, if you so choose."

"Why?"

"The stipulations of the will—"

She narrowed her eyes. "I am aware of the stipulations of the will, but why are you offering up the use of your plane?"

"Because you have work to do. Do you not?"

"I think we should probably make the team aware—"

"They're aware," he said. "After all, the board had to approve the marriage." He took a sip of his coffee. He seemed so unbothered she wanted to shake him.

"You've already talked to them, haven't you?"

"Obviously. I have told everyone that they are to expect a visit from you this week. I will accompany you, of course."

No. She needed distance from him. She didn't want it, but she needed it, and him going with her to New York was just...no.

"Why? You've never had anything to do with the day-to-day running of the business."

"I haven't, you're correct. But neither have you. And I want to make sure that everything runs smoothly."

"You don't have previous commitments of your own network to deal with?"

"Cameron owes me roughly a decade of service. If I wanted to show up at nothing for the next ten years he would simply have to take it on the chin."

She waited for him to move on to the next thing. To at least acknowledge that last night things had changed between them.

"So... That's all you have to say?"

"Was there another conversation you wanted to have?"

"Yes. There is," she said, staring at him hard.

"About the sex, I assume."

"Yes, Apollo," she said snappishly. "About the sex."

Why not be blunt? Why not say it all? She'd had the man on his knees in front of her with his face buried between her thighs. Where was the benefit in being missish now?

"It won't happen again."

"Did I say that I didn't want it to?"

"I didn't ask you. You got that out of your system and now it's time for us to move forward."

She was angry, mostly because that was exactly how she had thought about it initially, but how dare he say that to her? It was painful, and it felt mean. It felt entirely unfair.

"I don't... I don't understand how you can just say that."

"Hell, I'm your guardian. What happened was wrong."

"You're my *husband*. You're the one that took Rocco's place at the altar. You're the one who changed things between us. You can't sit back now and claim that you're only my guardian. Not when we took the vows. I'm not going to let you do that. Put me back in my place because it's what makes you feel comfortable. You made your choice, Apollo. Your choice was to do this."

"Are you honestly suggesting we live as a real married couple?"

For some reason, those words made her want to retreat. "No," she said. "No."

"I didn't think so. So you will see how things must remain the same between us."

He paused for a moment. "I do want to be very clear that was on a transaction."

"It didn't feel like one," she said.

"Good."

"But you know, you're the one who said some really hurtful things about it all. So why you should care now, and why you should be so concerned with what I think about it is beyond me."

He paused and a strange expression crossed his face. "I suppose that is still about me."

"I guess at least you have some self-awareness."

He lifted a shoulder. "Some."

"You told me attraction was easy. Cheap."

"I did. Because I didn't want you thinking anything about my attraction to you."

He was staring at her, his gaze meeting hers unapologetically, and yet there was shame there. She knew that. It was the strangest thing. Apollo was usually so unapologetic in every way, and yet this seemed to be skirting not only an apology, but an admittance that he'd been wrong in some way. "Is it true then? What you said to me about being attracted to any woman?"

"No. It's not. It's complicated. Desire is common, especially for men. But cheap... No. Men will pay dearly for sex. And it is an interesting thing, I find, that something as easy for men to come by as desire is treated with such reverence. It is given priority over other appetites. Because men will start wars, destroy their careers, destroy their families, go into debt, and all for what? Sexual desire. So the truth is, I do not think anyone—a man or woman should rearrange their life because a man desires them, because desire is easily created. But at the same time, men will burn down worlds for the sake of it. It is very easy for a man to justify hideously wrong acts if they satisfy his immediate sexual need. What I said was a lie."

She tried to process that. It was an interesting insight, and true, she supposed. She might not be well versed in the nature of men, but she did know that men were prone to risking themselves personally and professionally to have their desires fulfilled. But she didn't know what that said about him. If that meant he had compromised himself deeply for the sake of sleeping with her, and if that still made it of little consequence. Because in the moment his need to be inside of her had been bigger than his caring about propriety.

She didn't know if she was flattered or insulted by it. But then, he hadn't connected it to what had happened between the two of them. Only what he had said to her at the club.

"Is that true of you? Are you in the habit of burning your world down to have sex?"

"No," he said.

"Honesty. Let's have that. Maybe for you things need to go back to how they were. But I don't think they can. You were my mentor, you were my guardian, and now you're my... Well, the things we've done, I can't go back. And so I need you to tell me, the truth. I need you to give me honesty, even if you could never give me that again, I think that you owe me that here and now. I think you owe me a little bit of truth with our coffee, don't you?"

"All right. You can have that. No. I'm not in the habit of burning my life down for sex. I'm too jaded for that. I have watched too many people burn the world down over it. I'm no longer able to lie to myself that if I do that I will find satisfaction on the other side. Because that's how that works. Men lie to themselves. This will be the last time. The best time. At least, they lie to themselves while they bother to continue on with the fiction that they are actually good people held at the mercy of something bigger than themselves. There is a point for many of them where they simply accept that they're debauched and that their own needs are more important than the needs of those around them. But for many, the lies continue. The justification. One last time. And then... And then next time they'll resist."

"What did you tell yourself when you had sex with me?"

"Nothing," he bit out. "I told myself nothing. I wanted you, and I failed in the task of resisting you. I was weak. I can't pretend otherwise."

"Am I supposed to be flattered by that?"

"No. As I said. Never be flattered by the desires of men. But you must know, I am never overcome by desire. It was rare. But it won't happen again."

"Why…"

"Because it won't. How do you see your life, Hannah? What do you want for your future?"

"I want to take my father's company and I want to run it well. I want to grow it. I want to prove that I deserved to be there all along. That I am in charge of my own life, that I know my own mind. That I am not a stupid, silly woman. That's what I want. All of that and more."

"And what do you want in your personal life?"

"What everybody does. I suppose. I want a family. I want to fall in love and have children and…"

"Not everybody wants that."

"No. I mean… I know that. And I don't intend to do it for a very long time. I need to get used to running the company before I go changing things again. But… Surely everybody wants to be loved."

"No," he said. "They don't. And that is what I need you to be especially aware of. I don't want that. I don't want it because I no longer believe myself capable of returning the feelings. I don't want it, and I don't ever want to be the source of someone else's thwarted passion. You don't know about my past."

"No," she said. "I don't. Because you won't tell me."

"It's obvious enough that my last name is Italian."

"Yes. But you're from Greece."

"Correct. My father was an Italian man I never met. He broke my mother's heart. And she never recovered. She looked for love everywhere. She was flattered by the desires of any man. She wanted to feel beautiful, she wanted to feel cherished, and men will say whatever they need to in order to take pleasure with an object of their desire, won't they?"

"Your mother was taken advantage of."

"More than you realize. She fell in love with a man who lived in Scotland, and when he agreed to bring her and me to Edinburgh, she agreed without hesitation. It never occurred to her that it might be a trap. It never occurred to her that the man might not love her because she wanted to believe it so damned badly. He pushed her into prostitution. Manipulated her."

Shock hit her directly in the midsection.

"That's awful," she said, and she could see the way that it haunted him still. She meant it. She felt... Immensely sorry for the young woman who must've had him, believing the best of the world at one time only to have her soft heart used against her.

"Is that why you're so psychotic about me?"

"In part, yes."

"And it's why you need me to know that what happened between us wasn't a transaction."

His shoulders got visibly tight, moving up toward his ears. "In a fashion."

"Why did you do it? I don't understand. You want me, but... Didn't it matter that it was me at all?"

He looked like he was at a loss, and she couldn't remember ever seeing Apollo at a loss before.

"Rarely have I slept with a woman that I know. I think perhaps I was somewhat affected by that."

"You mean you usually sleep with strangers and sleeping with someone you have a relationship with is a novelty?"

"I don't know," he said.

"Well, I'd like to understand."

"Why? To what end? There's no point going over any of this, *agape*. Perhaps it's because you are my wife. And that changed things for me."

"Well, I'd like to know how."

"I can't give you that answer. Because I don't know the answer. I don't... It was different. That's all I can say."

There was more. There was more to him, there was more to this, and he wouldn't tell her. He was hiding behind that icy facade, that insistence that he remain her guardian, that nothing had changed. Even though she had spoken plainly and said that for her it could never go back. Apollo didn't really listen to other people. He played by his own rules. She knew that. Of course she did.

He was determined to frustrate her, she could see that. Exhaust her so she didn't push him here. And yet... She wasn't sure what she wanted. For him to tell her that she was special? He didn't know her. Not really. They didn't know each other. What he had just told her about his mother was completely new to her. They had been part of each other's lives, but in a very distant fashion. He had been a fantasy object for her, but nothing more. It was easy for her to tell herself that she had loved him, but what part of him? His looks, his aura of power, sure. Those were the kinds of things that anyone could see from across a crowded room.

But the substance of Apollo was hidden from her entirely, and she had to wonder if it was hidden from almost everybody. He'd been through horrible trauma, she knew that. But that didn't make this hurt less.

That while he felt significant to her, special to her, there was no real evidence that he was. She knew him as well as anyone in the world who had read a profile about him. Except she slept with him.

He'd been inside of her. And to her that mattered, and to him it didn't seem to. Beyond the lapse of control, that was.

It exhausted her. Caring for a man who might as well be a wall. And now after hearing about his mother she hurt for him too and she was tired. So tired of caring so damned much when he didn't seem to care in return. At least not in the way she wanted him to.

Maybe that isn't fair. Maybe for him this is caring.

Well, maybe the way her father and mother had cared was love, but it still left her feeling like a lonely little husk.

Was it too much to wish that she might be cared for the way she wanted to be? Even once?

"So you really want to just pack up and head

to New York?" she asked, because she didn't know what else to say. Because she wanted to push the conversation further and she could sense that she was at a dead end with him. Maybe she did know him. For all the good it did.

"Yes. I will have your things prepared."

"You're not even going to let me pack my own clothes?"

"You're welcome to. If you like. You may want to begin asking yourself what the best use of your time is. There is quite a lot of work to be done."

"I know that," she said, snapping.

"Well. You may wish to start behaving like a CEO. Delegate the task that you're not needed for."

"How is it that I've somehow retained a babysitter."

"Many people would be pleased to have me consult them. They would pay hundreds if not thousands for the privilege."

"Well. They've never met you."

"So certain. And so sharp and pointy."

"Yes," she said, waving a hand. "That's me. Sharp and pointy and utterly ridiculous. Absolutely no merit to the issues that I have with this extraordinarily weird situation."

"If you'd like, you can go in and speak to

your manager about the fact you will not be working at your job anymore."

"Oh, can I? Thank you."

"Sarcasm doesn't suit you. You're far too intelligent for that."

"Well thank you for the most useless compliment of all time."

She finished her coffee, and she did go to work, quitting unceremoniously.

"I'd like to manage the property here," Mariana said. "If you don't mind. Because what I would like is to bring the whole team with me."

"Well, that's going to make Rudolfo angry," she said.

"Yeah, but he's a bad manager. So I feel like he's getting no less than he deserves."

"It's true," Hannah agreed.

"When can I start?"

"When I come back from New York. I laid the groundwork for you this week. Because I'm going to make sure that it's known we're going to engage in sweeping reform of the properties."

She wanted to park the big emotions, the complicated things, and focus on business. For a moment. It was an issue, but not one that left her feeling bruised.

The annoying thing was, part of what she wanted was to make sure that she could integrate the technology from Apollo's company into the properties. Which was likely something that he had long been waiting for. It was the best thing for the business, one of the things that would set them apart, and she knew that she would get the best deal out there. Their connection would make it advantageous for both of them.

It was annoying because he was going to get something out of this, and it would be cutting her nose off to spite her face to put a stop to it. She couldn't do that.

She was enmeshed with Apollo whether she liked it or not. And the problem right now was she wasn't entirely sure how she felt about it. What he had done getting the New York office prepared for her arrival was actually good. She wasn't entirely sure she would've thought of it on her own. What would marrying Rocco have looked like? She would've been given the money and the control, and how would she have handled it? She felt pretty confident and bold, because she had been thinking a lot about what she was going to do to improve the company. She knew that he had been irritated she hadn't taken a job at her father's company, but a lot of it had come down to wanting to familiarize herself with the competition before that wasn't possible anymore. Before her connection to the company made it so no one would hire her.

She was studied up on the history of the business, and what had happened in the years since her father's death. She had ideas, and they didn't come from nowhere. Her business in hospitality classes had given her a good jumping off point. But there was a lot she didn't know about managing teams and big corporations, and Apollo certainly did know how to do it.

The way that he had so easily finessed the board spoke to that.

Though, she thought it was funny. She didn't think she had needed him as a guardian for the last six years. Not really. He was actually the most valuable one now. Because she was fine when it came to dealing with her own personal life. Her studies, her own job, her own ambitions. But yes, she could admit that she was young. And that the responsibility she was taking on was a big one. And maybe a little bit that she had even rushed herself into it because of her anger. That was really annoying. Having to see that some of his concerns were valid, and that his help was appreciated.

She wouldn't be telling him that, of course.

But she was aware of it.

When she returned from her conversation at

the hotel, her bags were packed and sitting by the front door.

There was also a car waiting.

"We'll head to the airport now. We will land in New York midmorning their time. It will be a day we spend getting you oriented to the time zone, and then the following day you'll go into the office."

"I didn't realize that you had signed up to be my secretary," she said.

"If it's what you need," he said. "I am happy to oblige."

"I had no idea you were so accommodating. I feel like I wasted a few years of my life leaving that gem undiscovered."

He lifted a brow. "Is that your takeaway from this experience? That I am accommodating?"

She let the silence lapse between them as she realized he wasn't even going to humor her for a moment. She was tired. Of him. Of this. Of him not reacting when she was a mess.

She'd tried to focus on work. She'd tried to be sensitive to his revelation of trauma. But he wasn't trying with *her*.

So now she was back to wanting a reaction. Any reaction.

"Yes," she said, blandly. "That is one hundred percent my takeaway. You're a secret softie. I could tell when you held me and whispered words of affirmation after you took my virginity in your study."

And on that note she swept into the car and closed the door behind her.

CHAPTER EIGHT

HANNAH WAS SATISFIED at her view of his shocked expression on the other side of the glass. She wondered what part of that sentence he found shocking. If he hadn't realized she was a virgin she would consider that a boon of sorts. At least for her own sense of mystery and her skill set. She'd wrecked it now, of course.

But it was worth it for the shock value.

He got into the car, in the back seat with her and made a slow show of rolling up the divider between them and the driver.

"You were a virgin?"

"Who would I have slept with?"

"You've been going out most nights, it was completely reasonable to assume you might have taken a lover."

"Oh, dear. You were wrong," she said, knowing she sounded cheerful enough to make him grind his teeth.

"Why?"

"Were you wrong? I suspect because you're a mortal like the rest of us and just not always correct."

"No. Why were you a virgin?"

So did she go for honesty or continue being flippant? It was a tough call. But she remembered his moment of honesty with her in the kitchen this morning and she felt some of her rage drain away.

"Do you really not get it?"

"Do I not get what?"

"You can just say no, Apollo. You can say you don't get it. You don't have to engage in questions on questions to avoid admitting you're out of your emotional depth."

"You're a child. I'm not out of my emotional depth with you."

"That's so insulting. Also I know you don't believe it." She took a breath. "So, let's try again. Have you not figured it out yet?"

"No," he bit out.

"I'm a cliché. You're my guardian and I had a massive crush on you for years, which I'm sure a psychologist would argue has to do with childhood trauma and displaced daddy issues, who's to say? Either way do you really think I offered to give you a blow job in the streets of Athens because I just had the bright idea to do it as payment?"

He was staring at her, his eyes dark and fathomless. He did think that. It had never occurred to him that an offer of sexual contact might come from somewhere emotional. That was…a lot.

"Did you think I asked for a wedding night because I was hot and horny for Rocco and thought you'd be a good replacement?"

Two slashes of color darkened his high cheekbones. His rage was visible, even as his expression remained stoic.

"You did, didn't you? You thought I was using you as a stud?"

"I didn't say that," he said.

"But you think it, on some level. It never occurred to you that I'd wanted you before? That this wasn't a whim for me, or something random?"

"No."

He looked out the window and she saw a muscle in his jaw jump.

"Did it bother you?" she asked.

He turned to her, his expression fierce. "No. I told you what bothered me was the idea I might have taken advantage of you."

"Is it? Or were you afraid I was using you?" It was, perhaps, a crazy accusation to throw out. But she was feeling wild and a little reckless, and tearing off strategic strips of her pride seemed to be an interesting study in gaining some control.

You had to give some to get some, and all of that.

"You seem intent on pushing immaterial issues."

"That isn't a no." She cleared her throat. "So if you were wondering, I wanted you. I always did. I couldn't make myself want other men, and believe me I tried. It's one reason I wanted to get away from you. But that all got turned on its head so I decided to take what I wanted."

"And that was me?" he asked.

She looked at him, his expression utterly inscrutable. "Yes. I thought you must want me too, at least physically. And you know, I did think of what you said. About how cheap male desire is. But knowing what you told me this morning, it's making me rethink it. I thought I could make you want me and it would cost you nothing. It did, though, didn't it?"

He made a low, male sound. "I don't know what you want to hear, *agape.*"

"I'm not sure either. Maybe that you were affected by it like I was? Maybe that it was special. Maybe that you care about me, and you aren't just unmoved by it like it seemed you were last night when you sent me away."

"If sex were cheap, worlds wouldn't burn

over it. If it were nothing, a sexual assault would be the same as a slap across the face. It is not. If sex was meaningless, indiscretion wouldn't raze marriages, families, lives, churches, to rubble. Sex is dangerous. And it can be heavy, light, transformative. So I've heard." He stared straight ahead. He didn't look at her. "I was not unmoved."

His admission was heavy and she didn't know what to do with it, where to place it neatly inside of her heart. There was nothing neat about this. It didn't make her feel better, either. Not really. Because she couldn't guess what the landscape of his soul looked like, and she felt like she was trying to traverse terrain she couldn't see. Buried beneath the darkened waters of trauma he didn't want to share.

And fair, she supposed, because before this past week he'd been an authority figure to her—whatever she thought about that, and it wasn't very flattering—and now whatever he said things had changed.

Sex had rearranged them.

Everything they had been. Everything they were now.

Apollo was still a sheer rock face, and yet, she'd seen more vulnerability since last night than she'd ever glimpsed before.

"Did I hurt you, Apollo?"

He turned sharply. "As if you would possess the power to do so? And with such a medium."

"Well, I'm sorry if I did," she said. "I imagine nobody wants to feel used. Even jaded billionaires."

"You may rest, Hannah. I did not feel used."

She didn't believe him.

"That's good," she said. "Least of all, I hope you don't now. I hope you understand that I... It was my fantasy."

"Because you..."

"I like you. I mean, I... I liked you. Had a crush on you." She was underselling those feelings, but how could she tell him she'd thought herself in love with him? That even now it felt like a twisted version of something much, much deeper than a crush.

She hadn't known him, not really. He didn't know her, not beyond his need for her to be some token of redemption. How could you love someone you didn't know? Someone who didn't see you as an equal?

Even still, the feelings were...powerful. If they weren't, she wouldn't have had sex with him. She wouldn't have felt so wounded by the marriage. She wouldn't have told him she was a virgin, or that she cared for him at all.

He laughed. The sound filling up the car. "A crush. I don't know that I have ever been subjected to anything quite so anodyne as a young girl's crush."

That hurt. Even though she'd deliberately downplayed it, it felt so...scathing and mean.

"Well, that's probably because you say things like that. Young girls are prone to having their feelings hurt when grown men laugh at them."

He did not look abashed, and she felt that was pretty poor manners on his part considering she had just apologized to him and his own feelings.

"Excuse me, I was concerned about you."

"I did not ask you to be."

"Apollo..."

"You were the virgin, Hannah. Not me. And while I appreciate what you said, I do, and yes, sex is something. It changes things. It changes people. I agree to that. I believe that. I... I'm not wounded. I'm certainly not going to take juvenile feelings to heart."

"I would think that you might recognize that what passed between us was not juvenile."

"No," he agreed. "What passed between us was not. But surely you must understand that any emotional attachments you have for me are... Pointless."

That actually made her want to jump out of the car and swim into the sea. Because how could that be? Okay. Maybe she had never been so foolish as to fantasize that they would get married or have a family or anything like that. But the idea that feelings for him, all the way, were completely pointless after so many years of caring for him just felt… Sad. And it wasn't her she felt sad for. It was him. It was his inability to recognize that he had someone in his life who actually cared for him. Sure, they were spiky with each other sometimes, but he had always been there. He had been a constant. A safe space.

She supposed the real foolishness was imagining that any of those feelings went the other direction. Because why would they? It was easy to imagine that they could, but he really did just see her as a responsibility. A prize to win. A job well done. She had seen him as vastly more.

"Do you care about anyone?"

"Your interrogation will have to wait." At that moment they had pulled up to the private jet.

They were ushered out of the limousine and the stairs were lowered for their embarkation. They climbed the steps and instantly she was awash in comfort. For all that the vehicle was luxurious—because everything Apollo had was luxurious—the jet superseded it. It might as well have been a modern living area. With midcentury furnishings and stonework, that she assumed had to be fake, because surely there was a weight limit on something that had to be airborne.

There was a slim, highly polished wooden bar and gold light fixtures. The walls of the plane were navy and gold geometric design work.

It was lovely. But it would not distract her from the issue at hand.

"Okay. We boarded the plane. So let's continue."

"Cameron and I have been friends since we were boys. Your father trusted me enough to put you in my care."

"You said to me more than once that I was the only good thing you've ever done. So on some level you must have conflicting feelings about your relationships with Cameron and my father."

"Cameron and I helped each other survive. We have a trauma bond more than we have anything else. He is my brother. He is… He is a part of me in many ways. His pain is mine. I don't know that he will ever fully realize that. When he had his accident and concealed himself even from me, it was like losing a part of myself. And yet I felt his agony. I would not call it a friendship. It is something deeper than that."

"Your soulmate, perhaps?"

He chuckled. "If I were built differently, perhaps. He might've been. But it would never have been easy."

"My father?"

"We had business ties. He was a good man, your father, but I was using him for connections, and he was using me for mine. In the end, we did connect in many ways, but it was our isolation that perhaps brought us together the most. He knew that if something happened to him he did not have a long list of people he could ask to care for you. He didn't speak to his family, your mother didn't speak to hers. It was… Perhaps the same sort of thing as I have with Cameron. Lost lonely people who are isolated from everyone else in the world. Could find a measure of comfort in each other as a result. Trust. Because there is no one else. Because there is nothing else."

"And you wouldn't call any of those things friendship. Or even family."

"I don't have the understanding of that that you might. My own mother didn't have the strength to love me or protect me as she should. My own father never met me. I never made friends out of a desire to have companionship, but out of a desire to survive. So perhaps that is the problem. In the absence of comfort, you define things differently. It is not about how you feel, but about how you might live. And so I never knew a relationship that didn't bear a resemblance to a transaction."

She felt burdened by her own experience of love—or a lack of it. But what Apollo was telling her painted an extremely bleak picture of his own experiences. That made her feel…a little guilty. For wanting so much from him. If she was damaged by her experiences, how did she expect him to be any better?

She'd felt ignored. He'd been fighting for his survival. Had felt like every relationship was bought and paid for.

"I find that very sad," she said, her throat constricting.

"Then shed a tear for me, *agape*. But it will change nothing."

At that moment, the plane was consumed by motion and so was she. As it hurtled down the runway and propelled itself into the sky. Her stomach dropped, but maybe it was all related to him. Maybe Apollo was the inertia. It was possible. Maybe it was all her. Maybe everything in her had been so upended by these things between them that she had yet to recover. Her words were reckless, dancing on the edge of something she didn't want to admit to herself, let alone him. It was all fine and good to talk about crushes and girlish longings, and to ignore the fact that he had wrecked her last night in his study. And maybe even more importantly ignore the fact that she had clearly done something to him. It was why he was so set on keeping things the same after all.

Perhaps she did know him. Maybe not all the details of his life, but the substance of who he was.

But she was weighing the cost and benefit of hammering away at Apollo when he wasn't in the mood to admit the truth. Or worse, maybe he would. That was the thing. Of all the things he'd said, which she felt circled truth enough, she did not think that he had actually told her the most real truth of all. Whatever it was.

"Why does it matter to you if you're good or not?"

She asked that, because everything felt circular. She asked that, because she didn't know what else to say. She asked that because she still wanted to dig, but she was tired of talking about sex, her virginity, and getting into her own vulnerabilities.

"Doesn't everyone worry about their soul at least a little bit?"

"I'm surprised you're the kind of man who believes in the concept of the soul, if I'm honest. You seem like the type that might want to believe we are nothing but finite beings who live for today and then die. Take nothing with us, so we might as well embrace hedonism while we can."

He shook his head. "I don't believe that."

"Why?"

"Because I felt pieces of my soul die. I cannot explain it. I only know it to be true. Something has to exist to die. And yet I have pieces of it left. I'm certain of that too. But never more certain than when I look at you."

He was sincere. In that moment, there was none of the cynicism, none of the hardness that was often present in him when they spoke.

"And I'm your redemption?"

She'd found the implication of that upsetting before. But it had new weight now, after what he'd just said. But it still wasn't fair. Not to either of them.

He paused. For a breath. A beat. "In a fashion."

"That is deeply messed up," she said. "Since I'm the person. And I feel like it should matter, what I want."

"I never said it didn't *matter*."

"But your idea of what is right or wrong supersedes what I tell you."

"Not last night."

"Was it about what I told you, or was it about

you? I actually can't bear to continue to hammer at this if you're just going to insult me again. But I need to know... Did you want me? Or did you just want sex?"

"I wanted you. And it is the precise reason it will not happen again."

"That is also the precise reason we cannot go back. You're not my guardian anymore. And maybe you can't be my husband. But can we at least stand on equal footing?"

"That would be ridiculous. Seeing as I am a man with much more experience of the world than you and—"

"Fine. I can give you that respect. But you should also respect me enough to treat me as you would anyone who worked with you. Can we find a place between Lord, redemption arc, and wife?"

"All right," he said. "I can try that."

"Am I supposed to be flattered that you're willing to try?"

"It certainly more than I've ever done for anyone else."

She didn't think that was true. She wondered why he was so committed to the narrative that he had never done anything for anyone. That all his relationships were one-sided and mercenary.

She had always seen him as impenetrable.

And she wasn't sure how she'd imagined he'd gotten that way. That it was part of who he was. But she knew why she had become the Hannah that she was now. Doing her best to please because she had wanted so much to matter to people who she had difficulty getting attention from.

To the angry rebellious Hannah of the last six months who had been suddenly tearing into the narratives about her life. But she had never stopped and really wondered what had made him this impassable, immovable object.

But he had hinted at enough things in their past few conversations that she had to wonder. He had told her about his mother, about having to run away.

At one time he had been a sad, lonely little boy. There would've been nothing hard or mercenary in anything he had done. And yet, somehow, he had rewritten these things to make himself feel…better? Worse? She wasn't sure. She had never particularly wanted to dig into Apollo as a man. She had seen him as a fantasy object, as an obstacle, but never as a whole man. She wondered how many people ever did. He was rich and he was stunningly handsome. He was more than capable in all these ways, and with certainty, he never seemed like he needed any help.

But she wondered now. She truly did.

"Why don't you take some rest, little one," he said.

"Don't condescend to me, Apollo," she grumped, but she was feeling tired.

"Is it condescending to worry about your well-being? Tomorrow I will take you around the city."

"I'm from the city."

"How many years has it been since you've been back?" He asked as if he didn't know the answer.

"You know I haven't been since my parents died."

"I do. So it will be good to be home, won't it?"

She thought about it, very critically. She thought about Manhattan, and she thought about the estate that her family had had in Vermont. She wondered if either of those places would feel like home now, or if they would simply feel painful. Like a time she could never step back into. There had been a time when she thought of them simply. As happier days. And then she had gone and torn into all of it. Taking it apart piece by piece and she wasn't sure it could ever be put back together.

"You can use the bedroom," he said.

For some reason, she didn't want to. She

wanted to stay with him. Defiantly, she lay across the couch that she had been sitting on. "Apollo," she said sleepily. "How old were you the first time you went to New York?"

"Twenty-one, I think," he said. Except she could see that he didn't think, he knew. With precision.

"That young? I didn't think that you and Cameron really found your success until a few years after that."

"We didn't. But we had… A business of sorts. I went with a client."

"I see." But she didn't.

And she was starting to get so tired it felt like a fathomless sea threatening to pull her under. She couldn't see the bottom of his trauma. It was all darkness. She didn't know if she had the strength to swim into those depths just now. It had been such a long couple of days and the subtle movement of the plane over pockets of air was beginning to rock her to sleep.

CHAPTER NINE

WHEN THE PLANE touched down in New York, Apollo roused Hannah. She had slept for the entirety of the flight but he had not slept at all. She was such a strange creature. Digging and persisting into all these darkened corners, as if she was going to find something that would explain away… Him. As if she was going to find something that would give her answers about why he was the way he was. She wouldn't find them. He knew that. It was so simple, he would've untangled all the aftereffects of his youth a long time ago.

He felt raw. After the conversation they'd had and he didn't like that. He wasn't used to it. She might not guess at what he was talking about, but it forced him to relive it. It reminded him of the boy he'd been a long time ago.

Someone he didn't like to reflect on.

A young man who'd still been able to feel

guilt and dirt and shame and disgust over what he had done.

And vulnerability. When he and Cameron had first gotten into the business of selling their bodies, many of the others around them who were doing the same took comfort in illicit substances.

"What's the point of wasting the money we just made?" Cameron had asked.

Apollo understood why people did it, because he had wanted the memories to go away. He had traded himself for drugs just one time. But had felt sick with the feeling of failure after, and had only created a new memory he needed to hide from.

And that, he had realized, could be a dark road. One a bit too much like the one his mother walked. He and Cameron had made promises to each other. After that. They would maintain their control, they would run their own business, and they would keep their wits about them. It was important. So very important.

And gradually, he had learned how to manage his own vulnerability. Without the use of substances. It was just that he had never quite learned how to turn that off.

And if Hannah thought it would be so simple...

"Did I hurt you?"

He shoved that to the side. He had been worried about hurting *her*. That was all. Using her. Because he had been in the space of lost control when he had taken her, and that was singular.

In a way that he didn't wish to speak to her about.

"I like you."

Her words echoed inside of him, along with his own dismissive response to them.

It had been a hideously unkind thing to say on his part. But he didn't know what the hell else she wanted to hear. Something kind, he imagined. The kind words from him would do nothing for her in the end. Because it was nothing that he could maintain. It was nothing that he could spin into something of use to her.

No, he would continue on helping her. That was all he had to offer.

His business acumen. It was easy for him to imagine a world where the ties between himself and Hannah were finally cut. Where she went off on her own, and the only association they yet had was one made of business. But it made him feel adrift. And he hated that most of all. So he didn't spend any time on it. Instead, when the plane touched down he watched her ride sleepily. She was so stubborn. Curling up on that couch instead of going to the bed. He would've carried her to bed, but he feared he would've made a disastrous choice after that. And he had no intention of taking things to that place. Not again.

She'd done something to him. Something painful, something wonderful. He didn't want to experience either sensation so unfiltered ever again.

Even as he craved it.

His issues were his own. Getting that close to revealing them on the plane had brought them up to the surface and he wanted to protect himself.

But he could also see…

He had hurt Hannah. Her father had hurt her. He might want to keep his distance, but that didn't mean he wanted her hurt.

All he had to do was redouble his defenses and he could get back onto better footing with her. Not the same footing they'd been on before.

If she wanted…if she wanted him to treat her like a person he could do that. She was offended by him seeing her as redemption, though for him that meant something. Even if she couldn't see it.

But he wanted her to see it.

Surely he could do that without revealing more of himself?

Hannah was still rubbing her eyes when they

disembarked from the plane and got into the limousine that was waiting for them.

"Maybe being jet set isn't for me," she said.

"Some good strong coffee will fix you up nicely." He smiled. "Unfortunately, it will be difficult to find here."

"It's New York," she pointed out. "You can find whatever you want here."

"Spoken with such confidence," he said. "But I find most coffee in America lacking."

But he took her straight to his favorite place in the city, a small hole-in-the-wall that served an eclectic mix of European delicacies. They had baklava and very strong espresso sitting at a tiny table right next to the window, against the busy street. Hannah's eyes were wide and searching as she looked all around.

"What?" he asked.

"I've never been anywhere like this."

"You cannot mean that. You grew up part-time in the city."

"My dad wasn't one for tiny cafés. Especially not…"

"Is this a bit downmarket for you," he said, feeling amused.

"No," she said. "Not at all. It's just different."

"I see. And you and your friends in Greece never went places like this? Not to banish her hangovers."

"No. Mariana is a very good concierge, and she got us into very fancy places. Plus, I'm actually not big on drinking. I did a little bit of it when we went out, but I've never had a hangover."

"Never?"

"No," she said. He felt both envious of her right then, and a bit regretful. Like he had somehow been part of holding her back from interesting parts of life. But also… He wondered what it would've been like to be so protected. To have had choices about these things. Real choices. He had made decisions, difficult ones, it wasn't as if he had no agency in his life. But his choices had been all bad at different points in his life.

Hannah had been able to retain a certain amount of innocence in a world that was unkind to the naive. Part of him wanted to congratulate himself for that, but another part of him knew he could take no credit for it. Not really. Her parents had established that boundary of safety. Something she didn't seem to understand.

He watched as she took a bite of her baklava, a stray bead of honey left on her lips.

He wanted to touch them, to kiss them away. But that wasn't who they were. And it wasn't what would happen going forward.

"Your father did love you, you know," he said.

Softness wasn't a native language to him. But he wanted to try and give her something. All of her actions these past months had demanded what he didn't know how to give. He could at least give her this.

"I know," she said. "I know he did. That's why the things that he did that I don't understand, the things that hurt me, hurt as badly as they do. If he had been awful, if I doubted that he and my mom cared for me, then… I wouldn't be so regretful about not having time with them. I wouldn't feel left behind. I wouldn't… It is that I loved them and they loved me that makes it hard."

"They died before they could finish with you. And I don't have children, obviously. I don't suppose you ever really finish with them. In the fullness of time, they might have made it up to you. The things they did back then. Because they were good people who would've listened to you if you would've said that you wanted things to be different. Your father set that trust up for you with the care and concern of a man looking at a child. Not a woman. He didn't know who you would become, and he never got to see it. Have some forgiveness for him. Think of how much you've changed. He might also have."

She shifted in her seat. "I never thought of it that way."

"I tried to help my mother," he said. He didn't know why he was telling her this, except he wanted her to know. The difference. The difference between parents who loved their children, and those who saw them primarily as a burden. And who could never, ever re-examine their actions because it was far too confronting for them.

"I'm a billionaire. I could change her life if she would let me. But for her to allow me to do that would mean admitting that things in her life are not all that they might be. And she cannot do that. She can't and she won't. I tracked her down in Edinburgh and she refused me. She said that I was just coming back to lord my status over her. She acted like I thought I was better than her, because I had always thought that I was better than her but... We were the same. And she knew it. Your father loved you. My mother grew to despise me. I was an emblem of everything that had ever gone wrong in her life, and she made sure that I knew it. She was too filled with spite and hatred to even allow me to help her."

"I'm sorry," she said. "I really am. You didn't deserve that. No child does. Every child deserves... They deserve to be loved. To be cared for. And I realized that my parents did care for me. But I was lonely. Perhaps if they'd lived until I was older, I would have known how to tell them that. Not that I did a great job of telling you."

I'm sorry for the part that I played in your loneliness," he said.

"It was probably for the best that I got sent to boarding school. I was *less* lonely than I was living at home, even though at the time I resented the change. So in that way, I think you helped. Apollo... How did you get out? What... What happened?"

"That is not a conversation for baklava and espresso and very small cafés."

It was perhaps not a conversation they ever needed to have. But he could feel his resolve to keep it from her wearing thin.

Everything he'd done with her in the past had either produced quiet capitulation or later, rebellion. And she was right about one thing, all of that had been about her occupying a symbolic place in her life. Talking to her, spending time with her, he was beginning to see something deeper.

Lonely.

They were both lonely.

She had hooked into something within him that he hadn't even known was there.

It was strange. And entirely unwelcome. He was used to having control, and she... She stripped it from him. It would be easier if it was only in the realm of sex. But here in this little café, she made him question his own resolve, and that was something he didn't have an excuse or reason for.

"Let's keep you moving," he said. "You want to stay awake until bedtime."

One thing he was certain about, it would be best if they stayed busy. Best if they were able to stay out in public. Because for all the promises he'd made himself about not wanting to touch her again, he could feel himself weakening there.

He did not wish to be weak.

"Will I?" She asked as they swept out onto the street.

"Yes," he said. "And tomorrow when you have to go into the office you will thank me."

They decided that they would see each other's favorite places. And that meant Hannah taking him to The Met, Central Park, and the Magnolia Bakery. While he showed her a gritty art gallery that he had grown attached to as a pretentious new enthusiast of art in his mid-twenties.

She spoke with broad hand gestures about each art piece they stopped at, and her enthusiasm was something more than infectious. Perhaps the thing that hit him hardest was…his own enthusiasm for the art seemed to affect her.

They passed by St. Patrick's Cathedral, and he hesitated.

"Do you want to go in?" she asked.

He felt frozen to the spot. And seen in a way he wasn't used to being seen. He was supposed to be sharing his favorite places in the city but he hadn't counted on this. He hadn't even thought of it, really.

"Come on," she said, linking arms with him and propelling him toward the large wooden doors.

As an architectural marvel, it was stunning. All ornately carved gray stone in the midst of the steel and glass of the city. Archaic to some, he supposed, and yet to him, it had created a stillness within. He had been compelled by it, from the first. He could remember being a young man and wondering if he could still go into a church after everything he'd done. Then he'd remembered his mother always had her rosary, even after everything, and he'd decided that he would go.

He touched the holy water when they walked in and made the sign of the cross, a reflex. Hannah didn't, but walked in with him. "I've never been here," she whispered. "My dad had no use for churches, and my mom even less."

There were people kneeling, praying, lighting candles. He reached into his pocket and took out a folded American hundred-dollar bill that was there and pressed it down into the slot of an offering box. He'd come in and lit candles in here before he could ever afford to make the suggested offering. He felt compelled to give now, for himself and for anyone else who might need the candle and have nothing to give for it.

"What's that for?" she whispered.

"Payment," he whispered back.

God knew that was too honest. But they were in a church. A lie felt like a sin. A funny thing, that he should concern himself with adding another sin to his vast list.

But here, he always wanted something different.

Just as he did when he was with her, he supposed.

He walked deeper into the building, feeling small beneath the arched ceiling, the massive pillars, and soaring stained glass windows. It had been a comfort then, feeling so insignificant and new. He wasn't sure what it was now.

She held his arm as they walked through, past the kneeling faithful, and back out onto the street, so loud and busy it was like the silence of the cathedral had never been real.

"That's one of your favorite places?" she asked.

He felt…exposed in a way the art gallery had not made him feel. "Yes. The first time I was in the city I felt compelled to stop in. My mother would take me in every cathedral we passed to light a candle when I was young and… I felt like I ought to. I remember I walked in and there was an old woman, kneeling and praying, her dress shabby, her shoulders stooped. A man in a sharp, custom-made suit knelt down beside her. I was struck by the image, that both were welcome. I thought perhaps then I still was too."

"Why wouldn't you be?"

His chest felt twisted up. "By then my life had become complicated. I was not the man I'd hoped to be. But there was something…healing. About knowing I could go there, light a candle. Be in the silence. It's like all the hymns that were ever sung are still in the stone. You can feel it." Perhaps she'd think him insane. "Or at least I can."

"I feel it too."

He worked to lighten things after that. He took her to a Mediterranean restaurant with a glorious dining patio, where you had to queue up out front and pay only with cash. Followed by a walk through The Village.

"I used to wonder what I would have to do to be able to live a life here. There was something so quiet about it. I think it was the first time I really understood that in the middle of a city like this silence costs a premium. A well-preserved home on an old street means you've made it."

He could still remember wandering here when he'd had his free time. Imagining another life. He was living that life now, he supposed, but it didn't feel quite like he'd imagined.

"Did you ever buy a place here?"

He shook his head. "No. By the time I could afford it I wasn't so romantic. This isn't near my office. Therefore it isn't practical. And anyway, I chose to make my primary home in Greece. Perhaps because it felt like taking something of myself back. I never asked to move to Scotland. I didn't ask to lose my life, my language. That is the problem with being a child, whether your parents are good or not. They make decisions on your behalf. On that, I think we can connect. They choose what they think you need. Or perhaps what they think they need, and you get no say."

It was getting late and the streetlights had come on. They were charming and old-fashioned, though to him, they didn't seem so old. He was from one of the very cradles of modern civilization. With history stretching back so far it was nearly impossible to track.

And still, something about this place would always call to him.

He had never shared these truths about himself with another person. Her favorites were very much New York to the eyes of a child, while his... They were a mix of his missing home, missing his soul, his desperate desire to be part of a class he wasn't. His hunger to escape the scarcity that had dogged him for so many years.

His need to be forgiven.

He wondered if she could see that. Did he want her to? What was the point of it, except that when faced with the idea of not having her in his life at all, he found himself feeling adrift. She was an anchor he had not realized bore so much weight in his world. Though he had to wonder how much of that was just his dislike of change. Of losing people. There were spare few people in his life. And he had attached a great deal of importance to Hannah.

She was his new church, in that sense. The thing he looked at which made him ache. To be whole. To have a soul.

Dieu, he'd told himself he would keep himself separate today. Forever.

But just as the cathedral had enticed him to his knees, to a position of what some would call weakness, Hannah made him vulnerable.

Being finished with her, setting her free, that would be the fulfillment of all the good he'd ever done. And so in truth, it would be a good thing to let her go. In a year's time, when the marriage could be dissolved, he would feel glad about it. And not wistful in any way.

Wistfulness was the province of other men.

As was vulnerability.

They had walked a near impossible amount, and when they arrived back at his Upper Eastside penthouse, they were disheveled in a way he rarely allowed himself to be.

"Well," she said, sinking onto a chair by the expansive windows in the apartment. "I feel like we've done enough."

"Do you think you've defeated jet lag?"

"I do," she said.

When he looked at her sitting in the chair, he could only see that night.

When he had dropped to his knees before her and tasted the sweetness between her thighs.

When he had sunk inside of her beautiful, tight heat.

He had told himself that he wouldn't think

of her this way. He had told himself that he wouldn't think of that at all.

And yet, he was.

"I like you."

"Did I hurt you?"

He gritted his teeth.

"What?" she asked.

"I didn't say anything," he said.

"I know you didn't," she said. "But you're looking at me with questions in your eyes."

"I don't have any questions," he bit out.

"Then were you just thinking about the other night?" she asked.

He could see that in his mind far too easily. Could see her, naked and glorious and the redemption he wanted most.

"It was last night," he said.

"Was it? I slept on the plane. And we did change a time zone so I think... Never mind."

"Yes," he said. "Never mind. Because it is nothing."

"It isn't nothing. You said so yourself. It changed us. If it hadn't, today would never have occurred."

That was an unerring truth, hitting him square in his soul.

"You say that with such confidence," he said, his throat going tight.

"Well. I know it's true," she said.

"I don't know how to love anyone, Hannah."

Oh, he wanted…so much. But he was ever a sinner wandering through a cathedral. A man who wanted to glimpse a holiness he could never find or feel.

He said it because he had to be honest with her. He said it because he didn't want her to spin fantasies out of this desire between them. And yet he was desperate. To touch her. To hold her. To have her. It was so far beyond his own experience that he had no idea what he was supposed to do with it. When it came to sex, he had done it all. But it was mercenary. Void of any kind of connection or emotion. With her he had tasted something new, and it had opened up the space inside of him that had been untouched all this time. It had led to today. She was correct about that. He had shown her those pieces of himself that he had never really even trotted out and examined for his own benefit.

But he had done it for her. He had done it because of her.

He wanted to taste it again. This electric, deep connection that he had never allowed himself to have with anyone else.

He could remember the first time he had taken a lover because he had chosen it. Because he wasn't going to pay, and even that had been something twisted. It had not been about connecting with another person. It hadn't truly even been about pleasure.

For him, the act had been so tortured and deformed throughout his life and she… There was something about her. About the genuine strength of their connection that made it feel like it was his first time. And he hadn't wanted to admit that.

He had gone to great lengths not to admit it.

But exhausted from the day, from the years, from holding all of this for so long, he didn't possess the strength to deny it. To deny her. To deny himself.

"I didn't say that I needed you to love me," she pointed out.

"No," he said. "You didn't. But I will not lie to you. I don't…" He wanted to find words. But he didn't have them. He didn't know how to articulate this thing. This desire to connect with her while protecting himself. While making sure she knew that it couldn't become… He had no family.

He had no vocabulary for connection. He spoke so many languages, and couldn't figure out what he wanted to say in any of them. But his chest felt like it was raw and bleeding. His control stretched thin. Because he had been trying to deny himself since he had left her that night, and it was only getting harder and harder to do.

Sex had never been something he'd had to resist. It wasn't about control.

But this wasn't a transaction, and it wasn't about proving himself. It wasn't about the freedom to take sex for free, rather than charge for it.

She was so beautiful it was painful. And yet, she was Hannah, which was painful in and of itself.

He had no words.

All his resolve, all the lies he'd told himself to this moment didn't hold. He had no defenses at all. And he'd walked himself right into this place. Where there was nothing but her. Nothing but wanting to be in her arms again.

To find that place of refuge he had been denied all of his life.

To find that pleasure he'd never known.

That connection he'd thought lost to him forever.

He'd laid a snare for himself to be caught in, and he had stepped into it willingly and even now knowing that, he was nothing more than a raw, bleeding mass of feelings. Of desperation. A mastermind of his own destruction.

"Help me," he said.

They were torn from him, from a place inside of him that he hadn't known existed. They were horrifying, and yet they were honest.

"I want to help you. With whatever you need." She put her hands on his face. She looked at him, their eyes meeting. Intense and long. A deep, shared moment that transcended anything he had ever experienced before.

He looked at her. And he could only hope that she could read what he was trying to make her see. She kissed him. He growled, wrapping his arms around her waist and pulling her up against his body. This was what he wanted. This was what he needed. She had made him feel that night, and he was desperate to do it again, no matter how much he told himself that it was all going to go back to the way it had been before. No matter how much he had told himself that it had to.

He needed her. He needed her like air. He was reminded yet again of the time that he had tried illicit substances to try and change the way that he felt.

She was that.

A drug. A heady hit of something that he had long denied himself. But he had never felt as good as he did that night in her arms. And it really had so little to do with physical pleasure. With orgasms. It was more. It was her.

Because he knew that sex, stripped of its

soul, stripped of its intent, could make you feel more alone than anything.

But not her. Not this. Touching her was like holding fire in his arms. And it warmed him, all the way through. She was the most beautiful woman he'd ever seen. And he wasn't certain how he had been blind to that all this time. Something had changed. Well. She had. She had become a woman, and he had been intent on ignoring it. For as long as he could. Perhaps because on some level he had known that it would be dangerous to him. To his redemption arc.

But she wanted this. And he felt... He felt very like he might find salvation in this. Perhaps that was one of those foolish things that men told themselves in order to justify their need for release. He didn't think so. Because this felt more profound. Because it felt deeper. Because it felt more significant. More important. Or maybe he was just the same. As every client that had ever shelled out money for his time.

But she cared for him. She had said so.

He wanted to touch that. He wanted to taste it.

For just a moment, to know what it was.

To be touched because she liked him. To be kissed because she felt something. He didn't know how to feel those things. But the temptation to claim all that for himself was deep. Real.

He had made for himself a world where he didn't need anyone. Not their help, not their money, not their touch. He had made himself a fortress, because before he had to make himself the product. And he had earned that right. That solitude. That ability to stand alone. And yet he felt at seeing now. And perhaps it was inviting the past into the present. Perhaps it had been a mistake to show her all those things. To tell her how the hymns echoed inside his soul.

The way his memories of the two strangers who prayed together lingered.

Maybe it was his own fault for showing her that street he'd once dreamed he might live on. Because it brought her too close to the man he'd been, and that meant it brought him too close to that man.

So he kissed her. Because kissing had always been a game. Because touch had never meant much of anything, but now it did. It did. And what then? What then when he was so consumed by need and desperation, and the kiss did not allow him to retreat?

That's what he was looking for. Oblivion. This perfect, detached oblivion that he often found during sex and could not find it with her. She was the moment. And she brought him right to it. She was everything. Heat and light and innocence. Glory.

And what was he but a man with dirty hands smoothing them over all of this? He did not deserve it.

Did you think I was using you?

That tender question. He pushed it away. Because it got closer to the heart of what had left him seared after their sexual encounter. The sense that he might've been used again. And the shame that he hadn't been able to put a wall up. That it had been real.

Because did he tell himself that every time?

That it wasn't real. It wasn't real because he didn't care about them. It wasn't real because he didn't want them. Because think distant thoughts or even take a pill designed to create physical arousal and perform and so what was happening didn't mean anything. If he could go to a place in his mind where his body was off acting of its own accord, then it wasn't real.

And perhaps, part of him had fought against making any of it real.

For so long that it was no longer an achievement. The achievement would be a connection.

And yet with her… It had been there. Even if it was still behind a layer of glass, because he had been…

Conscious of the fact that she had perhaps wanted Rocco and not him.

But not now. Not now. Her touch was tender, delicate, and yet it was close to pain. It burned his skin like fire and yet he wouldn't have her abandon him. Because he wanted it. He wanted her. "Touch me," he demanded, rough. He began to tear his own clothes off, impatient. For her hands against his skin. For all of it. Everything. She did, her breath coming in short, sharp pants, her movements jerky and uncertain, and he planted her hand against his bare chest and looked directly into her eyes. He knew that she had no idea what was happening. Between them. Inside of him.

He had a hard time understanding it and it was happening within him.

But she wouldn't know. Of course. She knew nothing about him. Not anything real.

He would have to tell her. But not now. Because he wanted this. All of this first.

If that made him a selfish bastard then that's what he was.

But he wanted this moment. She had seen him. In the church, she had come this close to seeing him as anyone ever had. Anyone besides Cameron.

She wanted him. Him. And it wasn't about a cold, dead transaction that came down to lust.

It was something deeper. And just for now, he wanted it. She had lost her virginity to him. And he wanted this for himself. This one time knowing she wanted him. Cared for him. He wanted to be there. All the way.

She wasn't dressed as a seductress this time. Not wearing her white lace. She was dressed in a sweet sundress, one he had seen her in all day, and when she stripped it off she revealed simple pink cotton underwear beneath. She unhooked her bra and flung it off to the side, revealing pale pert breasts to his gaze. She was lovely. More than that. Beautiful. The kind that reached down deep and struck a chord in a hidden place inside of him. The kind that left nowhere for him to hide. And perhaps even more notably made it so he didn't need to.

Then she was naked before him. He could feel the way that made her vulnerable. She looked soft. Lovely and untouched. In spite of the fact that he had touched her everywhere that first night they were together.

It was a mirror of his own soul. And he realized now why he'd tried so steadfastly to hide it. All that he was. All that he had ever been.

Because the stark truth of the two of them standing there, naked, regarding each other was almost too much to bear. And yet he must. He looked her in the eye, and moved toward her, taking her hand, as he had done on their wedding day. He squeezed her, and then moved to her, putting his hand on her cheek and lowering his head so that he could kiss her. She was glorious. Everything.

And when she kissed him it was that sweet promise of all the gentle things that he had never had in his life.

A taste of what normal might've been.

The anticipation of summer. The night before Christmas. Getting a new puppy. Knowing that when you went to bed that night someone would be there with you, holding you. All these things, these little things that he had never had. His mother had gambled with his childhood, but he had bartered all that he might have in adulthood for...

For all of this.

For this penthouse and this view. For the chance to own a house on a street he'd never even bought a house on the end. Because later he hadn't remembered. Later it hadn't mattered. But the street was still there. And so was St. Patrick's. And there was something strange in that that he couldn't quite put his finger on.

As if all the chances weren't spent. As if he could still go back.

But all of his thoughts were eradicated when the kiss between them became deeper. Harder.

And he did not retreat to a deep place inside of him, rather he was lost in the moment. The heat and fire between them. The slick ride of her tongue against his.

She might not be experienced, but she was enthusiastic. And she more than made up for any inexperience with that.

He put his arms around her and crushed the infinitely lovely creature to him. Hannah. Who was all passion and fire and familiarity.

He picked her up, and carried her determinedly into his room. He wanted her on a bed. He wanted to do this properly. He wanted to do this like he hadn't before.

He brought her into his bedroom and laid her down across the bed, her gloriously lovely body on display for him. He growled as he regarded her. She was simply stunning. Unlike anything he had ever seen. Art living and breathing before him. And he told her so. In all of his languages, to try and make up for his inability to speak earlier. To try and make up for everything. Because he was a miserable guardian. He was the worst man for the job, it turned out. Because the biggest monster out there that he should've protected her from was him. And here he was glorying in her. Taking from her to satisfy this beast inside of him. This needy, desperate part of himself that could no more turn back now than quit breathing.

But he kissed her. Her lips, her neck, down her breasts, and then between her legs. He pleasured her until she cried out. Until her fingernails dug into his shoulders. Until their passion created a new space inside of him. Not to hide in, but to glory in.

This was raw and real. There was nothing between them. Their skin was hot and slick with sweat, their hearts beating hard. She was Hannah, who he had known for half her life. And he was Apollo, who she knew as a friend of his father's. She knew in this strange, broken form he had fashioned for himself.

They had lived separate lives. Served separate purposes. And it was almost a miracle that they came together like this. Primal and urgent and filled with need. Miraculous, even. The way he was desperate to taste her, touch her. The way her cries of pleasure fed something inside of him. The way her own needs surpassed his own.

He hadn't realized. Because he had not truly understood all that sex could be. The purpose of it. The point of it. No. He had never truly understood. Until now. Because it mattered that it was Hannah. And it mattered that he was Apollo. Because it was more important than the final climax. Because sex was more than bodies. Because it involved your soul. And he had kept his own back for so long that he understood isolation more than connection. But here he let it all be free.

When he slid inside of her tight wet heat and she called out his name, it was a healing prayer. And they blended together. Into one. One flesh. One heart. He let his mind go blank. He let himself feel. All of it. Everything. A white-hot blaze of glory that left him burned from the inside out.

Because this was altering. This had changed him. He would never be the same after this. After her.

He welcomed it.

Because she liked him. Because she wanted him.

And because he had been alone for a very long time.

She arched beneath him, her breasts pressed against his chest, her hands moving over his back. He brought her to climax, touching her, tasting her, moving within her, whispering dirty promises against her mouth. And then she brought him over with her.

For one blessed moment, all was still within him. He was with her. Their bodies were pressed together, their hearts beating in time.

But there was no thought. There was nothing before, and nothing after. There was only them. And he was not alone.

He knew then that he needed to tell her.

CHAPTER TEN

"I WILL GET you an extra blanket if you want," he said softly, the aftermath of their lovemaking still evident. They were breathing hard, his own heart beating erratically within his chest.

"No," she said, moving against him, pressing her breasts to his back. "I'm fine."

"Good."

"Are you okay?" she asked.

He laughed. "I suppose I am the one who should ask you that. Given that you were the one who only just had sex for the second time."

"I'm not the one who looked like they were drowning inside of themselves only a few moments ago."

"Is that what it looks like?"

"Yes. It is," she said softly, and yet it was ruinous. Because it was only the truth, and he couldn't deny it.

He still felt raw. From the way that they had just... From the heat of it all. The connection of it all. It was far beyond his own experience. And there was no physical act that he could not claim expertise in. But this had been unique. Because it had not been about skill. But about something much deeper.

"You know," he said. "I think to understand much of what happened today, and much of what you've seen from me, and even the reasons that your father chose me to be your guardian, there is something you need to know. I have been in business with Cameron since I was about fifteen."

"You have?" There was a question in her voice, but he could feel the weight of it. She wasn't naive. Not really. And he knew that she had already worked out he'd undergone a fair amount of trauma. Hell, he told her some of it. But he knew she hadn't quite figured this out, even if she was skirting the edges of it.

"Yes. We... That is to say, there was a certain point where we realized we could make a fair amount of money selling ourselves."

"Are you saying what I think you are? That you... That people used you for sex?"

She didn't sound shocked. Or perhaps that was a gift. She was gentle, it didn't sound angry. She sounded... Sad, perhaps, but resigned. Maybe that was what happened when your parents died when you were sixteen, and you saw the harder truth in the world. Maybe you could expand to accommodate many such truths.

"Yes," he said. "We both… We both came from difficult circumstances. I was dodging predators already for half my life. I felt like it was only a matter of time before it was all taken from me by force anyway. I decided… I decided to get ahead of it. We were petty thieves before that. I looked young for a long time. Cameron was tall. It was often my job to charm. To make people pity me. While Cameron would rob them. But… As I said. I was quite pretty. And I did look young. And I hate to tell you this, but that is an asset."

"God," she said, the word torn from her. "That's… It's awful."

"It is. But if I had the choice between being a victim and making money off what I had available to me then I was going to make money. We protected each other. Made a network. Eventually, we graduated from seedier sorts of dalliances to wealthy clientele. Hard-earned connection after hard-earned connection. I was with a wealthy client the first time I came to New York. A woman. Her name was Sandra Fielding. She liked a little bit of company along with sex. She wanted me to be a bit more cultured."

"And she... Treated you like a pet, didn't she? Something to make her loneliness more bearable?"

"Yes," he said. "And if I have one strength it's that I am very good at taking a step back from a situation I don't want to be in and making myself distant. So when things became too difficult for me, I would simply go somewhere else. But I stopped knowing how not to do that, Hannah. Whenever I have sex it's like I'm standing at a great distance from my partner. Until you. And everything in me craves the connection, and yet it's deeply uncomfortable for me."

"I wish I would've known. I... I would've been more... I would've taken it slower."

He had to laugh. At the role reversal. At the way she was treating him like he was the virgin.

"Do you find me different now? Do I disgust you?"

"No," she said. "Why would you? You did what you had to do to survive."

"That's a lie. Many people survive without selling their bodies. I wanted to do more than survive. I wanted to escape. All of it. But you know, I've been living under the delusion that I'm better than my mother. When I'm not. I didn't fall in love with any of my clients, but that hardly makes me better. I fell for the lure of easy money. And once you step into that bear trap you cannot get out of it. With connections, and some investments from Sandra we eventually started the tech company. She was our first major backer. So even in that, it's all sex for money. Sex to get where I am now. So when I tell you that I know sex is not just a handshake, it comes from the fact that I treated it like one for a number of years. At great cost. Do you know how afraid I was to step through the door of that church. Because I hadn't been in one since I..."

"Your mother still went into them."

"Yes," he said. "She did. I decided that I could too. For that very reason. I think I just wanted to feel like maybe I wasn't so broken."

"Did you... It doesn't matter but..."

"You want to know about my clients?"

"A little. But it feels wrong to ask."

"There are more men willing to pay than women," he said, his tone stark. "And I... I am in no way attracted to men. But I do like money. So yes. I did a great many things I did not especially wish to do. And you cannot walk away from situations like that without feeling violated."

"Have you ever talked to someone about this?"

He couldn't help himself. He barked out a laugh. "Like a therapist?"

"Yes. Like a therapist. This is complicated. It's like… It's like untangling years of sexual assault."

"It's not," he said, the denial coming harder than he intended it to. Because he had admitted, even in himself, that there were certainly aspects of it that felt that way sometimes. But for some reason right then he felt the urge to deny it. "I put myself in those situations. I agreed to do those things. Nobody forced me."

"It's a bit more complicated than that, I think."

"Maybe," he said. "But I could never afford to allow it to be complicated. I made my choice, and I kept it in the past. Back then I thought it was worse whatever the consequences might be. And so now I am left with the consequences. But also money."

"Apollo," she said, her voice so filled with compassion that he wanted to reject it. And yet he needed it. "I don't know what to say. It's just… I am so sorry that you were alone. And that you had to… That you felt it was your only choice. Because whatever you say now, I do believe that then you must've felt it was the best and only thing you could do."

He could remember feeling that way. Feeling like he was spinning his wheels. And the amount of money he had gotten offered by some guy in an alley had changed things for him. He had finally seen a way forward.

"I think there are other people who can handle such things better. Cameron is one of them. I'm not saying he isn't his own mess. He is and always has been, but he was never quite so wounded by what we did. I was. It went against my nature, and… I violated myself, Hannah. And it is something I have to live with. I traded myself, my soul, for this life."

She put her hand on him and he resisted the urge to remove it.

"You didn't trade yourself for anything. You're still here."

"Not the way that I used to be. This is a version of me. But nothing more."

She nodded slowly. "I think we're always changed by the things we go through. But that doesn't make us someone different." She moved closer to him. "I know that you're the one that is supposed to take care of me. And I know you're so much older than me, and honestly, you have lived through so much more. But… You're more than that. You are not going to be that forever. You have to forgive yourself."

"It isn't that easy." It didn't shock him that she couldn't understand. It wasn't a matter of forgiveness, but acceptance. He had proven himself to be the same as his mother, really. And that was the thing that he had to live with. The stark reality of his own weakness. Of the truth that he was no better than the woman he had spent quite a long time despising.

His parents were people he could never truly respect. And he had no evidence that he wasn't ultimately cut from the exact same cloth.

Maybe that was what bothered him most of all. "You haven't explained, though. How it connects to my parents."

Discomfort lodged in his chest. He had talked to her father about this, when he had first made the provision for Apollo to be Hannah's guardian.

"This all seems very out of the blue."

"I trust you. You understand."

"I do. But... Nothing is going to happen to you."

"Hopefully it won't. But if it does, I want you to take care of her. When the time is right, you can explain. Because when she's old enough, Marcy is going to tell her."

"She doesn't have to. She's made it out. She's done well. There's no reason—"

"There is. You know why. Because she needs to be able to protect herself. From the people

that would take advantage of her. You want the ones you love to learn from your mistakes."

"I met your father at an event six years or so after our company became very successful. And around the time of Cameron's accident. We met because I had struck up a conversation with your mother. She and I... We recognized each other. Because we had both, at different times, seen each other at events where we were the paid companions of the ones we were with. You know your own kind."

"What?" Hannah sat up, clutching the blanket to her chest. "Are you saying that my mother..."

"Your mother was an escort. For some years before meeting your father. Your father never paid for her services. They met, and fell in love. He didn't care what she had done in the past. And she loved him enough to let go of everything. She loved him enough to let go of any of the pain she might've still felt about it. She loved him enough to let herself be free. Maybe she loved herself enough. But we... We had a bit of a bond. I suppose. Instantly. And your father was so afraid that I was going to judge her, when he realized that I recognized her that... Finding out the truth about me always made him feel like your mother was safer. Having me around. He wanted that for you too. He wanted me to keep you safe because he felt like I understood the way the world works. That I could protect you from the reality of it."

"I can't... I can't believe that."

"Are you angry?"

"Yes," she said. "Because... Because my mother is dead and I never got to know this about her. Because we never got to talk about it. Because I didn't really know how they met. Because I didn't really... I never knew them. I never knew them, and they never knew me. I'm just... I'm angry about it. I don't understand why they had to go off and go canoeing in a river in Africa instead of... Instead of being home with me. We could've been the ones having this conversation and... If we only would have had more time."

"You wouldn't have been left with me."

"No. Maybe you wouldn't have been my guardian. Or maybe you and I would've gotten to know each other and it would've been normal."

"I would never have made friends with you. Because I don't make friends easily." He paused. "I traded in my chance for normal. It was not the death of your parents that created a strange situation for me. Whatever you believe, believe that."

"Well, it is what created one for me. I just...

I hate this. I want to talk to her about it. I want to ask her why. And you don't know why, do you?"

"No," he said. "But I can tell you that I do know your mother was a wonderful person. Lovely and caring, and always kind to me. She never acted like I was bringing old pain to her doorstep. And she could have. She allowed me to have a friendship with your father. And no, you can't know why. Except I can tell you the reasons are probably similar to mine. When you have no control in your life you make strange bargains. You do whatever you can to try and make something work for yourself. And you tell yourself you're going to get out, but I will tell you, your mother and I are exceptions. Because it is so hard to be done with that. With the money that it gives you."

"My mother married a rich man. I guess that's an easy way to get out."

He shook his head. "Your mother fell in love. There is nothing easy about that. There is nothing easy about that when you have spent years searing your conscience and your soul. Trust me. Because I don't know how to love. I don't know how to put all the pieces of myself back together that I pulled apart so that I could find it in myself to figure out how to play those games. Your mother did the infinitely powerful and impossible task of surrendering her heart to another human being. Don't downplay it."

"I'm sorry. I just… I'm not upset about her past. I'm just… I'm angry at the universe, aren't I? Because plenty of people travel and leave their kids sometimes, but they don't all die on what should have been a lovely excursion. I've been in this place where I've been just blaming them. And being mad. Because I don't feel like they spent enough time with me. But the truth is, there would never have been enough time. And you are right. Time would've given us a different relationship. It would've given us more. And we didn't have that chance. And it's not fair. But it is. Same as I feel like I'm treading water. And I'm so tired. I'm searching and searching for something around me to hold on to. And it was never them. Because as much as I love them, it was never them."

"It is not me," he said. "I'm sorry."

"It never really should have been your responsibility to be."

"I think we are past responsibility, are we not?"

She shook her head. "I suppose."

"It is them that made you so angry these past few months? That caused you to rebel?"

"No," she said. "It was you. It just opened the door to allow me to be a bit bitter at them."

"Why me?"

She laughed, and rolled onto her back. He looked at her, at her gorgeous form and the smile on her face. "I wanted you. I... I cared about you. And I knew that until I dealt with that I was never going to be able to move on with my life."

"What does moving on look like to you?"

"This, I suppose. Minus the technically being married thing. Being financially independent. Running the company... I have to actually go and do that tomorrow."

"I'll be with you," he said.

"Yes, but that wasn't the idea."

"Was sleeping with me the idea?" he asked.

She tilted her chin up and barked a laugh. "Um. No. I absolutely didn't expect to sleep with you, no."

"Even when you were being an absolute brat?"

"I could see that you wanted me," she said, turning to her side. "But I could see that you were very mad about it."

"I was. At you. How dare you?"

But he didn't ask it with any heat or venom. How could he? There was none left in him. Not now.

"You aren't a monster, you know," she said,

softly. "I was angry at you because I was angry at life. I still am, a little bit."

"I thought you were angry because you liked me."

"That didn't help. I wanted to be normal, and on the one hand I do think having a crush on your problematically young and sexy guardian is normal, but on the other hand, I knew I wasn't going to be able to just go out and find someone and hook up. I was a virgin because I was preoccupied with you, and that was annoying."

"I am not a virgin," he said, his voice rough. "Far from it. But I've had the kind of sex that takes more from you than it gives back. For what it's worth, you've given something back to me. In that sense I am close enough to a virgin."

She smiled slowly. "I like that. You've always been good to me, Apollo. And I understand what you've been saying. You can't give me love. I'm not sure I want it anyway. I need to figure all of this out first, I think. But what if we took care of each other for a while? I think that would be nice."

"All right, Hannah. If that's what you want. I'll take care of you; you can take care of me."

He said it as if he was humoring her. When

in fact he wanted it. Deeply. He had never been taken care of, not once.

Lying in bed next to her was the closest thing.

He didn't want it to end.

But someday it would have to. He didn't have the stamina to do this forever. She was so firmly beneath his walls, and even now he wanted to close it all off.

Not now, though. Now he would coach her through her beginnings at the company. Now he would be her husband, not just her guardian.

He would be all of these things now, and set her up for success.

And someday, he would simply be a man she once knew.

All the better for her.

CHAPTER ELEVEN

HANNAH LOOKED OUT the office window, down at the bustling New York streets below. The last two weeks had gone well. Really well. Apollo had come with her on the first day, and done formal introductions in the boardroom. It had made sense, since the board knew him. Of course, it had been their job—sort of—to present a united front as a married couple. In many ways, she didn't actually think the board thought the marriage was real.

The whole thing had been chaotic enough that she didn't think it looked overly authentic.

And yet, the lines were beginning to blur.

At least, as far as she was concerned.

She was nearly thankful for the reprieve that she'd had the last few days. He had flown back to Europe for five days to deal with something that had come up in his and Cameron's company.

And so she was staying in his penthouse alone, going to work alone.

He would be back sometime tomorrow, and that was good.

She missed him. It was interesting, to feel the footing change beneath her when it came to their relationship. And it was. It had.

After he had shared the truth of his past, things had in fact changed.

He was different. In every way. The first time they'd had sex had been electric, there was no denying that. But since then, it was like a wall had fallen down between them. The time in the penthouse when he had looked at her with those dark, wounded eyes had produced an entirely new sort of dynamic between them.

He had described it as if he had lost his virginity in a way, and she felt awed by that. It was weird to get closer to him with the aim of independence. Because the entire point of all of this had been to create a life for herself that was independent of her parents, of Apollo. It didn't require her to step into the halls of her father's company. And she was still dealing with a lot of complicated feelings around the revelation he had given her about her mother.

In order to deflect the thought she decided to call Mariana. It was late in Athens, but she knew that Mariana would still be awake.

"How is everything?" she asked without preamble.

"It's going well. You're right, the mismanagement at the property is pretty profound. But I have found several ways to improve it so far. I was preparing a report to send to you."

"Thank you," she said. "How is Pablo doing in concierge?"

"Oh, fantastic. The guests love him. Rocco is getting on well managing the outdoor activities."

"Good."

She didn't really have hard feelings about Rocco. In fact, she wanted to prove it by giving him a job. They had spoken briefly last week. He had told her that he didn't ever intend to scam her. She believed him. She also believed that life was complicated, and it was possible that he might've been tempted to take advantage of her had the marriage gone through.

It was for the best that she had gone off with Apollo.

But she still wanted to honor the friendships that she'd made.

"How is your marriage going?"

She sighed. "It's not a real marriage."

It felt like it, though. Or if not perhaps a real marriage, a real claiming, conquering, and consuming rolled into one. She'd downplayed her feelings to Apollo because they'd changed. They were fiercer, stronger than ever.

And had more power to destroy her.

This marriage wasn't the shattered snow globe she'd first imagined it was. But it wasn't…forever either.

"So you didn't sleep with him?"

Her denial died in her throat. "We have."

"Hannah! How come you didn't tell me right away?"

"Because it all felt too big. It still does. And I know that it isn't a forever sort of thing. It's more just fantasy fulfillment. I mean, what's better than getting it out of my system?"

"Is that what's happening?"

"Yes. It has to be. He's complicated. And complicated in a way that I can't… I'm not going to be able to help him."

"What do you mean help him?"

"He's really damaged. By things in his past." She was not going to list what they were. "And I feel for him. I really do. But I have enough issues. And… I don't want forever with him. It would never work. You forget, I lived with the man… Sort of for many years. And it was like living with my parents. This kind of distance neglect. And even worse, that's how he is emotionally. And he's definitely able to connect in some ways."

"Sexually."

She didn't tell Mariana, that for Apollo that was actually a really big deal. In fact, she felt guilty allowing that to stand as something that could be made light of. It wasn't. Not for him. It was a big deal that he could let his guard down for sex. And maybe for a lot of men it wouldn't be. Maybe for a lot of men it would be as easy as chasing an orgasm. Apollo could separate that from his own desire, from his own feelings. And she appreciated that. She appreciated that meant something different to him. That it did something different to him. But she also knew that beyond that wall, was another wall. He had told her himself, and she wasn't an idiot.

"Yes. Sexually."

And in those moments she felt held. For the first time in so many years she didn't feel lonely. And she had spent so much time being lonely. But she knew that if she became dependent on him emotionally it would be just another jail cell.

She couldn't trick herself into thinking that it could be something else.

"Hey, I'm all for taking what you can get in a physical relationship. But you do need to be careful."

"How much more careful can I be?" she asked. "I mean, I am being realistic about it.

I'm taking on board what he told me. Which is that he can't fall in love. And again, I don't want him to."

"I just find that sometimes your heart gets tangled up in a way that you didn't quite expect, and then you end up feeling pretty bad about it when you went in with your eyes open and you still get yourself a bit wounded."

"I appreciate it. But I'm just going to keep doing what I'm doing. I'm focusing on the work. And I'll be back in Athens in a couple of months. I'll be able to do the work from there instead of being here."

"Is that what you want?"

"Yes. Greece is my home. In a way that New York just isn't anymore. I'm going to have to invest in a house here, but I'm going to get a place of my own in Athens. I think I'll feel… Whole. Finally. Like something is mine. Like it's coming together."

"What feeling are you looking for exactly?"

"It's like I need to take back all those years. Those years when I was living a life I didn't choose. Those years when I was lonely. My parents mandated loneliness to me. And I will never not be angry about that. Angry at them. I wanted… For a long time I wanted somebody to love me. And it was like I had to sit around and wait for it to happen. I'm never going to do that again."

"You have friends here," Mariana said. "And we love you. For all that we're a pretty ragtag group."

"I know you do. I appreciate it more than I can ever say."

"I would be your friend even without this job. You do know that, don't you? I know that you were stuck with the parents you were born with, and then Apollo was your guardian. I feel like maybe you're trying to create a situation where you force your friends to stay friends with you."

She paused. Because maybe it was true. Maybe in some ways she was trying to continue those friendships in the best way she knew how. Agreements and documents, because beyond the parental relationship it was really the only way she knew to reinforce things.

"Maybe I am doing that," she said. "Maybe this is me trying to make a situation for all of you that was made for me. And that isn't fair."

"No, because you definitely don't make me feel like our actual friendship is contingent on me doing what you want. You gave me choices. And I could've stayed at my job, and I know that you would have stayed my friend. Of course, this is a better job, and it's definitely more what I want. But I'm never going to use our friendship as an excuse to slack off."

That bolstered her. This whole thing had been such a confidence boosting experience. Because she didn't really need Apollo to navigate this job. She didn't need money to keep her friends. She could use it to build her life, and she could trust that she wouldn't have to live in that isolation again.

But then she thought of Apollo. And the furtive nights between them. The increasingly intense feelings that she had whenever he walked into a room.

It frightened her. Made her want to run away. But she also wanted to cling to it forever.

"When are you coming back?"

"I think probably I'll come back for a visit on the fifteenth."

"Great. Will make sure that we can go to dinner. And give you a tour of the property. I think it's already looking better."

"Great. I can't wait. I'll see you then."

She sat down at her desk. And mused. She and Apollo had a year of marriage left. In a way that was comforting. It would give her time. It would give her time to burn this thing out between them. To maybe figure out what the rest of her life looked like in a personal regard.

She'd been sitting on the truths about her

parents. About how the denial of time was the real enemy, much more so than them.

Her mother had been a prostitute. Her father the man who loved her, not in spite of it, but as part of who she was. To hear Apollo tell it they'd been so devoted to each other. They just hadn't known how to show her that same love, but it didn't mean they hadn't felt it.

They'd done the best they could at the time. And they'd never had the time to do better.

If they'd still been alive, she'd have told them what she needed.

Because she deserved to be fully loved.

She couldn't fix that with her parents but...

Maybe after Apollo.

She would date a nice man. One who didn't have all those scars in his past. One who wanted to give her...

Everything she'd been denied.

Without thinking, she called him. He didn't pick up.

She ignored the sinking feeling in her chest.

He was busy. And anyway, why had she called him?

It was so complicated. He was tangled in so many aspects of her life, and they had only made it more complicated, then they had married each other, and she had made it more complicated still when she had seduced him in the library.

She felt so powerful sometimes. The object of his desire.

Especially understanding what that meant.

She looked down at her phone, and then opened up a spreadsheet on her computer, trying to focus.

And that was when the door to her office opened.

There he was. Dark thunder and intense black eyes.

"What are you doing here?" she asked.

"I couldn't stay away," he said.

His voice was rough and filled with intensity, and it was everything she had ever wanted to hear. He couldn't stay away.

It was why he hadn't answered his phone. He hadn't been busy. He had been on his way here.

And right in that moment, a brilliant, bright light of need ignited within her.

He couldn't stay away.

It was all there. The truth of it. He didn't look at her like she was his charge. Didn't look at her like she was a ward to be taken care of. He looked at her like she was a woman, and he was a man who needed her.

He closed the office door, and turned the lock.

"Apollo," she said, looking around the highly

polished corner office, the windows facing other buildings and the streets below.

He pushed a button, and they didn't. She knew that they did that, a highly glossed film within the windows that would lower to make it impossible to see inside, but they could still see the outside world.

"Give yourself to me," he commanded.

"I…"

This was heat and fire, this was the opportunity to meet him. As equals. They'd made love more times than she could count over the past two weeks, but there were moments that had shifted things, moments that she couldn't ignore. That stood out in her mind. Of course the first time, had been about her. Her needs, her virginity. He had been skilled, and he had been good, but it had still been different than that time in the penthouse when he had begged her to help him. Because the feelings within him had been so foreign, so beyond his control, and so close to the bone that he had needed her to hold him. That had been about his desire. I desire that went beyond the physical.

And this?

This was about the two of them. Coming together with no walls.

But she had to be brave enough to close the

gap between them. Brave enough to banish the anxiety within her.

It was only a year. This thing. It wouldn't last forever. Why relegate herself to a corner of her own soul? Why consign herself to more loneliness?

It was inevitable. It had been a part of who she was from the beginning of her life.

She knew what was going to happen at the end of all of this. And whether or not she threw herself into their thrilling sexual connection, what difference did it make?

It would all be the same. In the end he would leave. In the end, she would ask him to.

They would divorce. Because it was the agreement. They would divorce, because they both had real lives to get back to, and they weren't these.

They weren't this.

And so there was absolutely no benefit to holding herself separate.

She began to slowly unbutton her shirt and let it fall away.

Then she unzipped her pencil skirt, and consigned it to the floor as well. She stepped out of her high heels, leaving herself so much smaller than him.

He watched her, the tension and color mounting in his face. She could see his arousal building. She moved to him, and gripped the knot on his tie, loosening it slowly, her eyes meeting his as she did. She had so many questions. Had anyone ever done this for him? Surely in the years since he had stopped being an escort he had women on hand to service him. To give him exactly what he wanted, and yet for some reason he had never been able to let himself be carried away by it. He had always been held back by those well-crafted defense mechanisms he couldn't disengage.

His trauma was more powerful than the need that he felt. But with them it wasn't. Maybe it was because he trusted her.

In that sense, she did matter. And she could take that. She could use that to soothe some of the loneliness inside of her. It was safe enough.

It was safe enough as long as it was sex.

Because like he had said, it wasn't a handshake. But neither of them were foolish enough to believe that it was love.

This mattered. It was emotional. And it was normal for her to feel things. It was okay. It wasn't something she needed to run from.

Slowly, she began to work the buttons on the shirt, exposing his well-muscled chest to her hungry gaze. He was the epitome of masculine beauty, but it wasn't why she found herself drawn to him. There were many beautiful men. Just like sculptures. You could look at them and feel an appreciation for the aesthetics of them, but feel no passion toward them. What they had was something else. Something elemental. And she grabbed onto that, and held it tightly, because it was perhaps the one thing that made her feel singular in this moment, in her entire life.

There were many beautiful men. Just like there were many beautiful women. But none of them had made him feel this.

And none of them had ever made her feel this.

This was something special between them. It was not a dispassionate, crude coupling simply about release. Though she wanted release.

She prized the journey. The hitch in his breath. The way his heart beat hard beneath her palm. The way her own heart rate sped up, and her breathing became shallow. The slide of fabric as she pushed his shirt and jacket from his shoulders. The anticipation she felt when his hand went to his belt and he began to undo it slowly. When he undid the button on his slacks and lowered the zipper, when he stood naked before her, well-muscled thighs and heavy masculinity sending her brain into a tailspin, an explosion of fireworks popping off within her.

They hadn't touched. Not really. She realized

she wanted something more than surrender. To give him something, everything.

And then he wrapped his arms around her and she pulled him tightly to her body, the feeling of his rough, hard body making her gasp. He was so glorious. And this was overwhelming. He kissed her. Consumed her. It was deep and hot and slick, and everything she could have ever wanted. She clung to him, and found herself being walked backward, toward those windows. He turned her sharply, her vision blurring as she looked down at the scene below.

"All of this is still happening," he whispered in her ear, smoothing his hands down her spine, down to cup her ass. "The world is still turning. Can you believe it?"

"No," she whispered, her breath leaving a cloud behind on the glass.

He kissed her neck, and pressed his body against hers, the cold glass making her nipples tight. She squirmed, unable to find satisfaction, and need building between her thighs.

He continued his featherlight exploration of her body, his lips on her shoulder, his fingertips tracing circles down her spine. Never touching her anywhere intimately. Never touching her where she needed him most. She could feel the hard, hot column of his arousal pressing into her rear, but he did not advance further.

He kissed her lightly, all over her back, knelt down behind her, his large hands cupping the rounded globes there, but he did not kiss her where she wanted him to, and he did not linger. He rose back up, slowly pushing her hair to the side, slowly running his fingers through the silken strands. She was shivering. Poised on the edge of a knife. Ready to come if he breathed too heavily. She was shaking. Violently.

"Apollo," she whispered. Making an even larger cloud against the glass. He moved his large hand around to her stomach, and pushed her back firmly against him, let her feel just how hard he was. She moaned, rolling her hips, seeking something. More of him. More of everything.

"Ask nicely," he whispered.

"You know what I want," she said.

"Yes," he said. "I do. And I want it too. More than anything. But you need to ask."

She breathed out, watching that cloud on the glass again. Then slowly, she lifted her finger, and began to write. *Please.*

He chuckled. "Please what?"

Slowly, deliberately, she wrote an *F.* And then continued with her request, which was bold and something that pushed her beyond her previously defined limits.

"I want to do so much more than that," he

said. "Do you know, I can't sleep when I'm away from you? I can't think. I don't understand how this happened. I don't understand how I've known you all this time, and now everything has shifted. Changed. I don't understand."

There was something about those raw, desperate words that actually terrified her. That pushed her to the brink.

But then she couldn't think anymore because he was kissing down her back again, lowering himself beneath her and spreading her legs wide. He licked her, right where she was wet and needy for him, and she gasped. As his tongue penetrated her slick channel, followed by his fingers. She pressed her palms against the glass and canted her hips back toward him as he moved one hand around to the front where he circled that sensitive bud between her legs as he continued to torment her with his clever tongue.

"That isn't what I asked," she panted, hovering on the edge of a climax.

"You want to end this, because you don't like to live in the space. I understand that. Because in this space, you're wrenched apart. The most vulnerable that you can be. Does it help you to know that I'm the same? I can't think." He licked her then, deep. She shuddered, coming apart at the seams, her climax tearing through her like a train.

Rending her asunder.

"Is it better now?" he asked.

"No," she panted. "You know it isn't."

"You are not my ward anymore. It isn't my job to coddle you. To take care of you. You promised that you would give me what I needed just the same as I gave it to you. So you have to prove it now. Don't get impatient."

He returned his attention to pleasuring her, and she ended up lost. Held there in space. Everything zeroed in on this moment. The dissonance of the whole world moving around out there, in plain sight, while she could fathom nothing bigger or more important than what Apollo was doing between her thighs, adding to the intensity of the moment.

There were no years between them. No gap in experience. They had become one creature, striving toward satisfaction. Striving toward completion. And more than that, reaching. For a connection of their souls. Because nothing else would actually satisfy.

He stood, and moved against her, pressing his hand over hers on the glass, and positioning his hardness at the entrance to her body. He wrapped one arm around her and held her tight as he thrust into her.

"Apollo," she cried out.

"Hannah," he growled in return.

Her body was pressed against the glass, the whole world spread out before her, Apollo at her back. It was like a metaphor for this entire situation, and for just a moment it pulled her from the glory of the pleasure that he was building within her.

It was the truth of it. The whole world was out there. All of the things that she could be. If she wasn't tied to him. If she wasn't continually tethered to the life that her father chose for her.

With what she had now she could do anything. Be anything. She could have as much day-to-day involvement in the company as she wanted. As much or as little. She could stay here. She could go back to Athens. She could go anywhere. She could take a hundred lovers or decide to take a vow of celibacy. All of it was up to her. Out there. And then there was him. Strong and solid at her back, moving within her, and he really was the other choice. Because there would be no limitless freedom with Apollo. She would be Penelope.

Waiting at home while he lived his life. Feeling hollow while she waited for him to figure out if he could love her in return. Truly.

The world or Apollo.

Herself or this all-consuming need that

would always demand that her feelings be tangled around him.

She knew what she wanted. Or rather, she knew what she wished she wanted. She also knew that in this moment, she had chosen him. For this time, she had chosen him.

Because the board didn't really believe that they were married, and there was no impetus for them to live together as man and wife. They certainly didn't need to play games in her office.

But it didn't feel like a game. It felt like he was demanding that she strip herself bare, deeper than clothes, deeper than skin. It felt like he was asking for her to give pieces of her very soul, and had she given enough?

Hadn't she given enough? To a man who had promised he could never love her, what would ever be enough?

Just don't love him. Please don't love him.

Maybe it wasn't love. Maybe it didn't have to be.

She repeated that to herself. An endless tattoo that rolled through her as he thrust inside of her. Taking her. Over and over again.

Just don't love him.

And then she could no longer fight the rising tide of need within her.

And it crashed over her like a wave. Endless.

Rolling on and on.

Apollo," she said, or maybe she only felt it. Maybe there was no difference, here in the space. Between what they said and what they felt. Maybe it all mingled together with real honesty, and pain, with real feelings that transcended language.

Just don't love him.

He moved away from her, and she turned to face him, trembling. "I have work to finish," she said.

"I will meet you at home," he said. She could see walls come down in those dark eyes, and she wished she understood why.

She knew that he was pulling away. She wanted to know why he was, but asking would defeat the purpose.

"About tickets to an opera. I thought you might want to go."

"Are you asking me on a date?" she asked, moving away from the window with trembling legs and beginning to collect her clothes.

"Yes. I am."

She had never really been on a date. She and Apollo had been sleeping together for well over a week, but she had never been on a date. She wondered if she ought to tell him no.

But you have a year. Just a year.

"Yes. I would love to. I just need to finish here."

"I have had a dress selected for you. It will be in your room waiting when you return. I have some business to attend to, so I will meet you. A car will drive you to the opera house."

"Okay," she said, uncertain what to make of all of this.

It was like the gesture of inviting her out was a step closer, but there were many other things that seemed like a withdrawal. She wanted to ask him. To what end? Because it would only be defeatist for them both.

So she let him pull away. She let him dress and leave. And she finished her work for the day and went home.

Home. This wasn't her home. She was going to buy a home in New York.

She thought of that beautiful street in the village. The one that he was so enraptured by when he had been a young man who had come to the city.

A young prostitute.

She stopped.

The truth of his past gave a new context to that story. He had come with a wealthy woman who was using him. Who had bought his body.

She really thought about what he must've

felt. Being part of that wealthy world without actually being in it.

And the church.

Wanting desperately for some kind of spiritual reconciliation but being uncertain of whether or not you could have it all the world around you was still so... Complicated. Broken. He had done some things he didn't want to in order to survive. To protect himself. To compromise himself to make himself safer in the long run, and she couldn't imagine what that must have been like.

She felt a crack forming in her heart. And it was letting all manner of tenderness in where he was concerned, and she didn't especially like it. It was better when she could push against him. Better when they could oppose each other.

There was so much pain in the world. Her own mother had experienced this same pain. Maybe it had been why she couldn't show Hannah the love she wanted. Maybe it was why Apollo...

She hated that they'd been hurt.

She hated that he'd been hurt.

But she was so afraid of him hurting her.

So afraid that the love she'd felt for him—always—was real, no matter what she tried to tell herself. About how she had been young, how she hadn't known him. That this new, all-consuming need was just that—need.

Because maybe if she could believe that, she could believe that at the end of the year, she would be ready to walk away.

The dress was beautiful. Blue and strapless and formfitting. Off the back, sheer fabric was attached at the shoulders like a cape that cascaded down in a shimmering waterfall.

On the dresser was a box, containing an elegant diamond necklace that glinted in the light.

She dressed and did her makeup, and went downstairs at the appointed time the car was set to arrive.

The drive across town was slow, the traffic in the city oppressive. But she took a moment to try and steel herself. To try and get her thoughts in order. To get her defenses back up. It was difficult to believe that only a couple of hours ago he had her naked and begging in her own office.

And now he was taking her to the opera.

The driver pulled up to the steps and she thanked him, getting out and walking up to the midway point. And then she felt heat gather at the base of her spine, and turned. There he was, standing near the street, wearing a sharply cut tuxedo, his gaze burning fire.

The crack within her heart widened. And she knew she was in trouble.

CHAPTER TWELVE

HIS RESOLVE WAS STRENGTHENED. Seeing her like that. Standing there on the stairs like an angel. A vision. The most extraordinary thing he'd ever seen. She was beyond belief. His Hannah.

She had been equal parts innocent and filthy today in her office, and he had loved every moment of it. He had done a lot of thinking while he was away. Or rather, the thinking had been done for him. He had not chosen to have her on his mind every second of every moment of every day when he was trying to work, but she was.

Things had changed. While he was working on his projects with Cameron he found himself wanting to call Hannah and ask her opinion. Because he valued that opinion. Because she was brilliant and clever, and he knew from watching what she had done with the hotel chain and just the weeks since she had taken over and implemented her plans, that she would bring about a fantastic partnership between their companies. He also knew that if he were to bring ideas to her about his own business, she would likely have insightful thoughts about them.

He respected those thoughts. Was curious about them.

He had gone to a restaurant he hadn't been to before in Paris during a summit that he and Cameron had to attend. And he had wanted to ask her what she thought about the food, and was annoyed she wasn't there.

He had spent so much of his life in relative isolation, and normally he was used to it. But it felt strange, wrong, even to experience anything without her by his side when she could be there.

More than that, it simply wasn't as enjoyable.

The lights from the opera house were gold behind her, and she was as lovely in that dress as he had imagined she would be. Madame Butterfly. A long-lost duchess. She could have been anything. But she was Hannah. His wife.

The ring in his pocket burned.

She had rings for her wedding to Rocco, rings that she had chosen beforehand, and he had not had one. He still was not wearing one.

He'd decided something while he was away. The marriage should not be temporary. The marriage should be permanent. They were better together. And no, he couldn't offer her love. There was so much inside of him, fractured in the dark, floating around in the endless black sea of his soul, and there was nothing he could do about that. He didn't love the idea of offering her a shattered mirror. He would rather she have something whole. But he was honest about it. He had told her. He felt that the overriding truth was that they were good together. Better together than apart.

And he was confident that she would see that.

They could conduct their business individually, and come back together.

In some ways, he felt that this was inevitable.

She had been part of his life for so long, and the idea of her not being in his life had never settled well. The image of what things would be like when she wasn't with him was just… He didn't like it. And he had lived enough life he didn't like. He was a rich man now, powerful. Why should he make compromises? He shouldn't. He should keep Hannah as his wife. That much was clear.

He walked up the steps toward her, and she smiled. He offered her his arm. "Come, *agape*. We have box seats."

"Of course we do," she said. "Luxury all the way."

"It is not luxury that I was concerned with, but privacy. I do not trust myself with you." There was a truth to that. One that went much deeper than sex. But she had done something to him. Peeled away the protections as if she had taken a knife expertly to flesh against the bone. Sex with her was not the same as sex with anyone else. He could let his guard down. He could let himself feel. He finally understood about connecting souls. It was like all the pieces of himself were united into one when the two of them came together, and it was unlike anything he had ever experienced before that. He needed it. He could not afford to lose it.

She was soft next to him, and she smelled like violets. He did not truly feel settled unless she was next to him.

Because every time they came together, it was harder and harder for him to put his defenses up afterward, and functionally he was now walking around the world without a shield. At least it felt that way to him. And that was her fault. So it was her responsibility to hold him together now.

"Are you all right?" she asked.

"Why wouldn't I be?"

"You're intense."

"Am I ever not?"

"No," she said. Then she smiled. "You aren't. So, I don't know what I'm worried about. Or why I said anything."

"I missed you," he said.

She stopped walking and stared at him. He couldn't read the expression in her fathomless blue eyes. He wasn't sure he wanted to.

"Thank you," she said.

But it wasn't *I missed you too*.

They continued on into the ornate building, and down the VIP hallway to the box seats. They had a private balcony to themselves with rich red curtains and plush seating. There was a fruit platter waiting for them and two glasses of champagne.

"This is beautiful," she said.

He was glad she thought it was. He wanted to take her out. He wanted to leave her in no doubt that for him, this was not the same as it had been. That there was no holdover to the guardian-ward relationship. She was a woman, and he was taking her on a date. She was his woman.

He didn't watch the opera, he watched her. As the notes soared, and the drama onstage built, he watched as her eyes filled with wonder. Watched as emotion took hold of her. Watched her throat work as it became clear the lovers in the play were doomed. Watched as her eyes filled with tears and one slipped down her cheek. And that was when he reached out and grabbed her hand.

She looked at him, and he felt pierced, all the way down to his soul.

She was the only person that he had ever intentionally built a relationship with. He had chosen to do right by her because he wanted to. And he had chosen to know her because he didn't think there was another choice. She was singular in his life. He and Cameron had been forced together by the whims of life, and he would have said that he and Hannah were much the same. Her parents had died. She hadn't chosen that, neither had he.

But in this moment, he had to wonder if this, this connection, was inevitable. If they would've always found themselves sitting here in this opera box. He would've had to explain to her father that things between them had changed. That it was different than he had planned. That of course he had never taken advantage of her when she was young, and never would have. But that he was rather blindsided by the connection between them.

Perhaps he could have talked to her mother about the ways that you tried to manage the scar tissue left behind by the sorts of wounds they had endured. It was something he could see clearly in that moment. That no matter the road they'd walked on, it would've ended up here. Unless he had chosen normal. Unless he hadn't ever sold his body.

If he would've chosen that quiet life in Edinburgh, then no. He wouldn't be here. He never would've been to New York. He would never have experienced world-class opera, least of all from a plush VIP private box seat.

And that was the tragedy. Because the only way to be with Hannah was to come to her broken. And the only way to be whole would have been a life where they never met.

He felt nothing but deep, profound sadness and regret. But he was going to ask her to be his anyway.

When the play ended, a sob rocked her shoulders and he leaned in, kissing her on the mouth. Softly.

"Are you all right?"

"It was very good," she said. "A reminder, though, that sometimes things are doomed. No matter how much she wished they weren't."

Did she mean them? He didn't like that. He gripped her chin. "I think things are only doomed if you allow them to be."

"I don't know. Sometimes I think there are forces at work that are simply too strong."

It was adjacent to what he had just been pondering. Fate. The fact that had he taken a different road he would not have ended here.

That the cost of this moment had been nothing less than his own hideous trauma.

And yet he was here. He could do nothing about that. He couldn't go back any further. He could only be here.

"I brought you out tonight because I wanted to show you how life can be. How things could be between us."

"What do you mean?"

"I spent these past days without you and I was miserable. I don't like being by myself anymore. I don't like going to cafés and not having you across from me. I don't like going to bed and not having you beside me. I want you in my life. I don't want for this marriage to be temporary. I want for us to stay together."

"What?"

She looked shocked. Confused. He reached into his pocket and pulled out two velvet boxes.

"One is for me. And this," he said, opening the next, and revealing a large, yellow diamond. "Is for you. I want you to wear a ring that I have chosen for you. Not one you chose to have a fake marriage to an Italian criminal."

"In all technicality, Apollo," she said softly. "Aren't you a half Italian criminal?"

"Yes," he said. "And my offer comes heavily connected to that reality. Believe me, I understand. Because as far as all that goes, nothing is changed. I am broken inside. I know that. I can't change that. But I do think that we would be better together than apart."

"You mean you would be," she said, as she reached out, her hand hovering over the ring. His heart stopped. And then she lowered her finger, moving away. "What does this offer me? I have lived life already with people who don't really love me. Or at least, can't do it the way that I want them to. My parents... They didn't give me what I wanted. Not ever. And you... You were my guardian, but you were never there for me. You were there for me financially, but never emotionally."

"Have I not been there for you these past weeks?"

"We had sex," she said.

"No," he said. "Believe me when I tell you, it is not just sex, and it is very different. Very different."

"I do understand that. And I'm not trying to minimize that. But I don't think it's a reasonable reason for the two of us to stay married. I have to choose. A life, freedom, or you. The same sort of thing that I have lived with always."

"I'm not enough for you," he said.

"No," she said, her voice jagged. "It's…it's the feelings that aren't enough. I can't just be a symbol to you. I already know that, because you have been my guardian for all this time, and it wasn't enough."

"Woman, I have given you everything. I married you so that you can have your trust fund, I helped you ease into the company—"

"I didn't need you. I didn't need you for that. I don't need you for this part of my life. I just don't. I finally have some sense of who I am. Some sense of what I can be. Disentangled from the past, and you are asking me to keep myself tethered to you, for what? Why does it need to be me?"

"Because I need you," he said. "Because you have unmade me. Because you have sent me to wander the streets without my defenses, and now you don't want to be with me? You were responsible for this. You have turned me into something that I don't recognize, Hannah. And you must do something about it."

"And what will you do for me?" she asked, her words fractured. "Will you heal? Will you do the work of putting all the pieces inside of yourself back together so that I can be loved. So that I can have what I need. Or will it be nothing more than torrid encounters in the afternoon and beautiful visits to the opera, and then I will sit in our house as lonely as I have ever been. Why would it be any different than all these years past have been?"

He stood, rage pouring through him. "It would be. It would be because I'm promising myself to you. And I am not a man who lies."

"I know you're not a man who lies on purpose. But what do you know about any of this?"

"I know that I spent years wishing that I could connect with someone. I don't understand what is happening inside of me. And you're the only person that can help me make sense of it."

"I'm not your emotional pack mule, Apollo. I have my own feelings. I have my own trauma. I have things that I need."

"And I am too broken for you."

She put her head in her hands, and the sound she made was pained. "I'm afraid you are. Because how will I ever know if you care about me, or your redemption? Am I a person to you? Or am I a symbol? I deserve… I deserve to be loved. I do."

She might as well have shot him. Straight through the heart. That heart that no longer had any protection. That was already so riddled with holes that it felt beyond help now. That it felt beyond healing.

"You are like everything else. Everyone else.

You couldn't actually handle the truth of my past…"

"It isn't your past. It's your future. You have told me exactly what your future is. To be a man who cannot love. And I cannot accept that. Why don't you get it. It isn't…"

"You said you didn't need my love."

"I did," she said. "I did. Because I don't see a future with you. So no, I don't need to love. But that's assuming that the marriage ends in a year. Just as we planned."

"If I divorce you your money reverts back to the trust."

The color drained from her face. "Would you really do that?"

He thought about it. It would be ruthless. Decisive. It forced her to change her mind, and it would give him the entire year to figure out how to manipulate her into staying.

He could buy her.

And that was when he let the ring fall from his hand and onto the floor. Because he had become that person. The one who would buy someone else's body. The one who would pay for them to be in his bed whether they wanted to be there or not. Because he was so broken, so damaged, he needed to take from another person in order to be whole.

Time and money had made him the thing

that he despised. He would turn her into his whore if he could. And nothing had ever terrified him more.

"No," he said. "I won't do that."

"I can't be alone like that. Not anymore. Please. Don't ask it of me. Let me go, Apollo. Let me… Let me make a life for myself that is nothing to do with you. Let me make a life for myself that is nothing to do with all of the things that have haunted me for all this time."

"Your father's company is good enough for you, but you must cut ties with me?"

"My father's company isn't a human being. It doesn't have the power to wound me. I'm not expecting it to have feelings for me, I just want to do a good job. I want the freedom to find someone who can love me. And maybe no one ever will. Maybe I will never be compelling enough, or interesting enough for somebody to—"

"It has nothing to do with you. The reason that I…" But he couldn't even say it. "I don't even know what love is, Hannah," he said, and he felt foolish, because he was a thirty-five-year-old man admitting that he had no concept of an emotion he was quite certain small children understood. But he didn't. He had no idea at all.

It was the thing that people talked about.

Wrote songs about. Poetry. It was something that concerned so many aspects of the world. The power of a mother's love was supposed to drive so many things and yet in his life it never had. Fathers were supposed to love their children and protect them, and yet his had abandoned him. Sex and love were supposed to be linked, and yet for him it had been tied together with money. With the basest of lusts.

He felt something different when he was with Hannah, but what was love?

Was it this feeling that he would die if she wasn't beside him? Or was it the need to let her go free so that she could be happy?

And if it was the latter, then did that mean it was enough to convince her to stay with him? Enough to give her a promise?

He didn't know. And he needed to figure it out. But he didn't know how to do it.

"I will go back to Athens," he said. "I'm sorry."

"Apollo…"

"You are right. This isn't healthy. It's not something I can ask of you. I'm older than you. And I have had time enough to sort through things that I have not managed to fix. It is not your job to fix them for me. And I am very sorry, Hannah. I should've turned you away when you came to my study."

"Don't say that. You shouldn't have I…"

"I should have. It was selfish of me. To take what you offered. I wanted it, and I wanted you. Being lonely is one of the single most terrible things in the world and I will not allow you to be lonely because of me."

He stood, and left the rings on the floor, not looking back as he walked out of the opera box.

She could only sit there, feeling devastated. What had just happened? She got off the chair and knelt down, picking up one of the rings from where it had rolled onto the ground. He had… He had proposed to her. Really. Truly. And she had… She turned him down. She had to. She had to. Because there was no way that he was ever going to stay with her. Why would he? He was an interesting, vital, beautiful man, and in her experience she was…

What was she? She was a lonely child who had never gotten past the isolation of her childhood. She was a lonely girl who had never been able to tell her parents how much she had just needed them to be there.

What is love?

He had asked her, and she didn't have an answer. Except it couldn't be this. It couldn't be the sharp, painful uncertainty. This plunge into the unknown. When she had imagined going off and living her life, taking over the company, doing whatever she wanted, going out and having fun with her friends, and being free to date, it hadn't felt sharp. Love could not be this painful.

And yet she felt like she was bleeding out. And she was afraid she loved that stupid bastard in spite of everything she had told herself. That it was a crush, that was all it was. That she knew better.

"Damn you," she said. "Damn you, Apollo."

Because she might as well be the doomed woman at the end of the opera, consigned to dying in a man's arms. When was it love or was it just a sickness over the chemistry between them?

How are you supposed to know?

She had been shoved into his sphere when she was sixteen years old and her crush had been incubated in the heat of her grief. How could she trust it?

How could she trust him?

She had done the right thing. She had done the strong thing. She was standing up for herself. She was taking what she needed.

Are you saying I'm too much for you?

She stumbled out of the opera box, the rings clutched tightly in her hand. She didn't see him anywhere. When she got outside, the car was waiting down at the bottom of the steps, and she got into it, half hoping that he would be there.

He wasn't.

She took her phone out of her pocket and she called Mariana.

"Mariana," she said, her voice breaking.

"What happened?"

"I don't know if I've made a mistake or not."

"Tell me everything."

Apollo walked the streets until the pain in his chest became unbearable. Until he had to stop because he was afraid he might be having an actual heart attack. He leaned against the wall of an old, ivy-covered building, surprised to find that he had wandered down to the village. He closed his eyes and shook his head. Was he doomed to be the same idiot, wandering around in the same places forever, never fully being part of them?

Because no matter how much money he had, no matter how much time passed, that seemed to be the case.

He called the one person who had always been there for him. "I need your help," he said.

"I've been expecting this phone call," Cameron said.

"What am I supposed to do? I want to be with her. But I'm… You know what we are."

"Yes. I know what we are. And I'm a monster on top of that, and I am with Athena."

"You're scarred. You're not a monster. It isn't the same thing."

"I wasn't referring to my scars. There are other issues. And she loves me anyway."

"Do you love her?"

"Can you doubt it? I love her with everything I am."

"What is it?" There was a total silence at the other end of the phone. "Dammit, Cameron, I asked you a question."

"I heard you. I just don't quite know how to answer. I'm sorry. I guess I don't understand quite what you're asking."

"No one has ever loved me, Cameron. I told her that I couldn't love her, but the truth is, I don't even know what it is. Is it this feeling like I'm going to die? And what good does that do her? Because she asked me that too, and it's fair. She wants to know what she could possibly get out of being with me, and I have no answer other than good sex. And you and I both know that well can leave you very, very dry."

"I love you, Apollo. Are you absolutely an idiot?"

That stopped him cold. "What?"

"What do you think our friendship is? And what do you think you've shown me in all that time?"

"We were forced together. We're more like brothers."

"Yes. Brothers are notorious for not loving each other."

"It isn't the same. I don't know my life without you. I didn't have to learn how to take care of you. I didn't have to learn how to put my needs second to yours when necessary, it was easy. Because…"

"Because you love me. Which I know is probably a very uncomfortable thing for you to have to hear, given the state of toxic masculinity in the world."

"I…"

"You were patient with me, and kind. When I was at my lowest, you didn't leave. When I gave you nothing, you gave to me extraordinarily. You were patient with me when many would not have been. When many would've tried to buy me out or get me away from the company because I was nothing more than dead weight. You were my friend. My brother. You demonstrated love to me. What do you suppose caring for her is? Love for her parents. Love for her."

"I've been trying…" He closed his eyes and

swallowed painfully. "I've been trying to find some path toward redeeming myself."

"From what? You cared for every single person in your life diligently. Without fail. You are one of the truest, most loving people that I know. If you need redemption, if you need forgiveness, it is not from anyone around you. It's from you, Apollo. I think you might be the only one yet who is not confident you deserve love."

"She said I was too much for her."

"Did she say that?"

"She was afraid she could not handle me."

"Listen to her. Don't take it personally. Listen to what that says about her own feelings. I love my wife, and she came with her own specific set of baggage. Sometimes her baggage and mine don't play nicely. And when that happens, she has to listen to me, to where I'm coming from and why I might take something a certain way when she doesn't. And I have to do the same for her. What is she really afraid of? I sincerely doubt it's you and your brokenness. She's probably afraid of loving you more than you love her."

"I don't want to live without her." He felt like he was staring into an abyss. "I am actually tempted to go and walk off a pier."

"Please don't do that. Please think about what you're saying to me. All the things in your life are worth less without her in it. What do you think that is?"

"I didn't like the café I went to in Paris because I wanted *her* there."

"If you don't even like a croissant without her there to taste it with you, I think you can pretty safely say you're in love."

"What do I do?"

Cameron laughed. "Apollo, you and I have been through some pretty hideous things. One thing we always did, though, was fight. To live, to grow, to have more. To have better. Don't fight any less for the woman you love than you would have for money."

"But... Money is only money. This is..."

"Nothing less than your whole heart. Perhaps you are too much for her. Perhaps you are damaged. But it would be better if you were honest. And said that you love her anyway. And then let her decide."

"That sounds painful."

"It probably is. But you should do it anyway. Because the alternative is... Wanting to walk into the sea."

His friend hung up then, and he simply stood there. He wandered the streets until the sky turned gray. And he found himself standing in front of St. Patrick's, just as the doors opened for the day.

There was no early entry or VIP. He came in with everybody else who was waiting to take their place before they went to work.

He thought of what Cameron had said to him, and as he walked deeper into the cathedral old words from his childhood echoed through him. He did know an explanation of love. It was patient and kind. It didn't envy, it wasn't boastful. It wasn't self-seeking. It didn't keep track of wrongdoing. It had seemed, to him, a list of impossible tasks. To love like that was to die to everything within yourself. And nobody could do that all the time. And what he had always seen as a barrier suddenly made sense to him. Every person in the whole world would fall short of such an ideal. People did it anyway. They loved and gave love imperfectly anyway always.

A shaft of sunlight came through one of the impossibly blue stained-glass windows, and it was like a light coming on in his soul. He was broken. But it didn't mean he couldn't love.

Cameron was right. He always had. The thing that had caused him to be the worst versions of himself were his denials of love. Considering manipulating her, making her his through blackmail, that didn't come from love, but from his need to deny it. His need to protect himself.

He knelt down on one of the cushioned

benches, his legs just giving out. And that was when he heard footsteps behind him. A figure knelt down beside him, and he turned. Hannah.

She looked up at him, her eyes glistening with tears. And then she pressed her head to his shoulder, her body shaking as sobs racked her figure. He held her. Until the storm between them subsided, because his own rose up like rain and poured from him just as it did her.

"It seemed like the right place to go," she whispered.

"Yes," he whispered. There were no declarations then, no words.

It was a prayer between them. And it joined all the hope, sorrow, and faith that had already sunk into these old stone walls. And something about that made him feel new.

They stayed there like that for a long time, and then he took her hand and brought her to her feet, leading her back outside. They had been in a cocoon in there, and all the silence dissolved the minute they were back outside, people on foot rushing around them, trying to get to work.

"There's a lot to say," she said. "But I suppose the most important thing is that I love you."

He closed his eyes, and he felt it. That he

didn't have to wonder anymore. What it meant. "I love you too," he said.

She didn't argue or bring up the fact that he'd said he couldn't do that. He appreciated it. But he wanted to explain anyway. "I couldn't understand the idea of love because I had decided that no one could love me. And that no one should. I am deeply ashamed of the things I've done. I felt like I had broken myself. That everything that was wrong with me was something I had done. It was a pain I had caused. And that meant I didn't deserve to be healed. If I had just gotten a job when I ran away from my mother, I would just be one of the many people in this world who had a parent that neglected them. I didn't. I made a different choice. The choices I made hurt me. They left me feeling used, they left me feeling assaulted. They left me detached from myself, and most of all, ashamed. I could not fathom love because I cannot fathom anyone loving me."

She shook her head. "I do. And I'm sorry. You were never too much for me. I needed… I needed to know you could love me. Because I spent so many years being lonely. While everyone prioritized their own needs over mine, I just needed to know I wouldn't be lonely like that again. I'm sorry I said you were too broken. I love you broken. I just want you to love me broken too."

"I'm just a fool," he said. "I didn't understand that I had everything I wanted. I just had to stop being so afraid. Had to let go of things that kept me safe. It's why I was different with you. Vulnerable with you. You made me feel that way all the time, and it made me angry. But of course it didn't occur to me that it was just falling in love. I'm not going to be perfect at it. Nobody is. But we can try. We can try, and I think that's the important thing." People from the streets kept going into the cathedral, moving around them. "Nobody that goes into those doors is perfect. It's all people trying. And I think part of me always wanted that. For my trying to be enough. And I was afraid that it wasn't."

"Your trying is beautiful. And it is more than enough for me."

"What about your freedom."

"Being with you can still be freedom. It only ever felt like a prison when I imagined myself still existing in that loneliness. I called Mariana last night. And I told her I was so upset with myself because I had gone and fallen in love with my first lover. And that wasn't responsible. It wasn't the right thing to do. She said what's the point of limitless freedom if everything you want out there means less than the thing you already have? I have the freedom to choose, Apollo. And I'm choosing you. I'm choosing this. Our love. No matter if we aren't perfect at it."

"Thank you." As declarations went, it wasn't a great one. It was just nothing more than the truth. From the bottom of his heart. Because he knew all about loneliness. They both did. And what neither of them had ever known before was this. And he was just so grateful.

He took her into his arms and kissed her.

He was going to love her. Forever. There was no doubt in him about that.

* * * * *

Did The Forbidden Bride He Stole *leave you craving even more passion? Then make sure to dive into these other stories by Millie Adams!*

His Secretly Pregnant Cinderella
The Billionaire's Baby Negotiation
A Vow to Set the Virgin Free
The Billionaire's Accidental Legacy
The Christmas the Greek Claimed Her

Available now!